"QUIET!" HUNTER SHOUTED IN A VOICE OF COMMAND THAT MADE BOTH OF US HUSH.

He then said, "Later we'll have a council of war. But the first thing to do is get the ship safely to sea!"

Already sails were dropping and filling with the night breeze, and already the *Aurora* was gliding away from the wharf. The moon went behind a cloud. I heard, or imagined I heard, the clatter of hooves from somewhere ashore. But if it was Steele, or Steele's men, they were too late. The *Aurora* and those who sailed on her were safe.

At least for the moment.

PIRATE HUNTER

The Guns of Tortuga

Brad Strickland and Thomas E. Fuller

ALADDIN PAPERBACKS
New York London Toronto Sydney Singapore

Affectionately dedicated to my middle son, Anthony Ramón Fuller
—*Thomas E. Fuller*

And to Amy, "the pirate's daughter"
—*Brad Strickland*

http://www.piratehunter.info

This book is a work of fiction. Any references to historical events, real people, or real locales are used fictitiously. Other names, characters, places, and incidents are the product of the author's imagination, and any resemblance to actual events or locales or persons, living or dead, is entirely coincidental.

First Aladdin Paperbacks edition March 2003

Text copyright © 2003 by Brad Strickland and Thomas E. Fuller
Illustrations copyright © 2003 by Dominic Saponaro

ALADDIN PAPERBACKS
An imprint of Simon & Schuster
Children's Publishing Division
1230 Avenue of the Americas
New York, NY 10020

Designed by Debra Sfetsios
The text of this book was set in Minion.

Printed in the United States of America
2 4 6 8 10 9 7 5 3 1

Library of Congress Control Number 2002108582

ISBN 0-689-85297-5

PIRATE HUNTER

The Guns of Tortuga

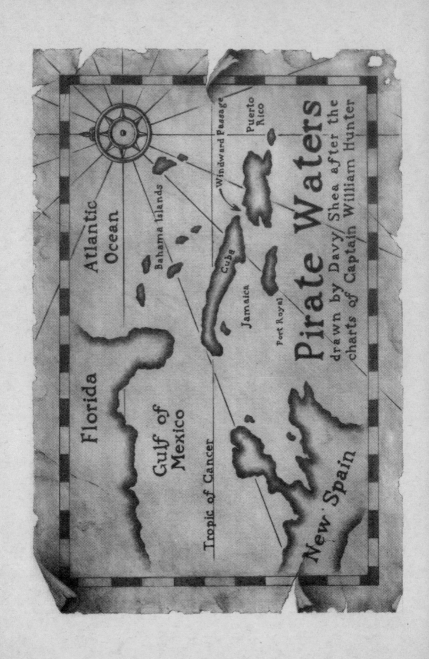

Main Mast

Mizzen

Fore

Rigging

Foretop

Captain's Cabin

Bow

Stern

Under the Pirate Flag

MY NAME IS DAVID SHEA, though I make do with "Davy." When my mother died of smallpox in March, 1687, I was sent to Port Royal, Jamaica, where my uncle Patrick Shea was a surgeon. In truth, we had a rocky beginning, but before long my uncle decided to make me his apprentice.

Two of his patients impressed me. The first was Sir Henry Morgan, the famous old sea dog. Though he had aged and become merely an ailing politician and planter, he filled my head with tales of buccaneers and booty. The second patient was Lieutenant William Hunter of His Majesty's Navy, recovering from grave wounds he had got fighting

Captain Jack Steele, the fearsome pirate.

When Lieutenant Hunter went back to sea, aboard the Navy frigate *Retribution*, my uncle shipped as surgeon, and I went as his loblolly boy. That meant, as I learned, a doctor's assistant. To my horror, Hunter led a mutiny against the stern Captain Brixton. He and the mutineers, including my uncle, were captured and sentenced to death.

But on the very day they were to hang, the twenty-odd mutineers escaped, and I was swept along with them, like a leaf in a windstorm. Days later we met Sir Henry Morgan once again. He gave us more men, nearly two hundred hardened old sailors, and the fine French-built frigate *Aurora*. Only then did I learn the truth: Hunter and my uncle were not really pirates, but pirate hunters. They had become mutineers as a disguise, so they could search out and sink the pirates that plagued American waters.

And sure, I joined with them, for an orphan like me had nowhere else to go. It was a fine life.

At least, it was until the morning we met the murderous big Spanish warship. . . .

CHAPTER ONE

Broadsides

"ROUSE YOURSELF, lad! That bloody fool Hunter is going to get us all killed, and I don't want you to miss it!"

My uncle Patch stood roaring in the open doorway, tall, massive, and looking as well groomed as an unmade bed. Groggy and disoriented, I tumbled out of my hammock and onto the scrubbed deck of the *Aurora*'s sick berth, for Uncle Patch—or Patrick Shea, to give him his proper name—was the surgeon of the vessel and I was his servant, the loblolly boy.

From the deck above, I could hear the pounding of boots and bare feet and the rolling of the drum as the crew rushed to their battle stations. This had happened before. In September 1687, Captain William Hunter had taken the *Aurora* from the former buccaneer Henry Morgan and had set out in it to be a pirate. Or so all the world thought. We on the ship knew that she was actually a pirate hunter, and her goal was to bring to justice Jack Steele, a deadly enemy to King James II of England and to all of His Majesty's ships and subjects.

Now it was January, 1688, and since September, we had taken five Spanish privateers, all of them small vessels that had given up without firing so much as a shot. The *Aurora*'s fame was growing, and it was Hunter's hope that before long Steele would come to believe we were pirates and so would let down his guard.

"Hurry, Davy," snapped my uncle again. "This time Hunter's caught a tiger, and he will neither let go of it nor show it a clean pair of heels!"

I shook my head and tried to clear it. In the distance, something that sounded like thunder boomed in across the sea. The shouts from above were now loud with laughter. I wondered about our crew, some of them navy men but most of them middle-aged retired buccaneers, friends of Henry Morgan's. What was it about danger that made them laugh so much?

"What is it, then? A navy ship? Or is it—" I babbled, tugging on my clothes.

"The Irish have a better command of language than that. Up and out with you! We'll have our work cut out for us when they start firing." My uncle had unlocked the cabinet that held his operating instruments and had begun to pull out trays with scalpels, pledgets, catgut, bone saws, and other equipment.

"'Tis unfair you are, Uncle! What is going on?" I have been told that I sound more Irish when I get excited, and perhaps it is true. Though I was raised in England, my late mother was Irish, and it was from her that I learned to speak.

My uncle set the trays side by side on a shelf he had caused to be mounted on the sick berth bulkhead. It was a tidy arrangement with a lip to keep the trays from sliding off when the ship rolled, and compartments that just fit the trays to keep them from moving back and forth when he was operating.

He turned to me, dusting his hands. "On deck! Do you not hear that bloody drum? On deck and all will become clear!"

Quick as thought, I was scrambling up the ladder to the deck. Everything looked just the way it had sounded belowdecks. Sailors were running back and forth, hanging from the rigging, shouting and waving their cutlasses. The ones not engaged in this manner were running out the guns on the *Aurora*'s starboard side, clearing the decks for action.

"Make ready, my lads, make ready!" rang out a laughing voice. Captain William Hunter stood next to the helmsman and the whipstaff, legs spread, hands on hips, head thrown back. We had been operating as pirates for nearly five months, but his appearance still seemed most strange to me. Gone was the elegant officer of His Majesty's Royal Navy that Sir Henry Morgan had recruited. In his place was the most piratical-looking fellow north of the Spanish Main.

William Hunter was resplendent in a long emerald green coat with red frogs and piping. His blouse and pants gleamed white, separated by the

4

yellowest silk sash its owner could find. And where he had found his hat with the ostrich plumes was still a mystery. Mr. Adams, the second officer, had speculated that the captain had a natural flair for the theatrical. What Uncle Patch had said barely bore repeating.

"That's it, lads," he sang out again, grandly pointing to starboard with his cutlass. "Run them out, run them out! Let's show them what we're made of!"

"We won't have to show them," Uncle Patch snarled as he clambered up next to him. My uncle looked more the pirate type than Captain Hunter, for he was a tall, broad-shouldered man who would have looked more at home in a boxing ring than standing over a patient. Looks can deceive, for he had a delicate touch and was well known as one of the finest surgeons afloat. He clung to the rail and stared into the distance, shouting, "What we're made of will be apparent to all, for it presently shall be spread all over the decks! Tell me now, are we really to attack that brute?"

Hunter threw back his head and laughed long and loud, an act that never failed to annoy my uncle. Indeed, I believe that is just why Hunter did it. I ran to the starboard railing and pushed my way between sweating and swearing pirates old enough to be my grandfather. Then I just stood there with my mouth open.

The thunder I had heard hadn't been thunder.

The sun was rising up out of the east like a burning orange, the sky deep royal blue, the sea almost black. And where the sky met the water, ships were fighting with flashes of fire, billows of smoke and, seconds later, the crash of cannon fire.

I strained with the rest of the crew to see what was happening. Three of the four vessels were sloops, or at least the one still firing and the one burning were. The only mark of the third was a sinking mast and men clinging to floating debris. And in the middle . . .

Hunter bellowed, "She's flying colors, Mr. Adams. See if you can make them out!"

"Aye, aye, sir!" Mr. Adams, who in his former days had been one of the oldest midshipmen in the Royal Navy, climbed the rigging to the maintop, whipped out his telescope, and scanned the battle. So did I, but from the deck.

The great three-masted ship unleashed another broadside into the burning sloop, sending sparks and burning wood exploding into the air. Whoever the men were on it, they were no cowards. With the ship burning and sinking from under them, they managed to get off one last broadside. I rubbed my eyes. Surely the shot hadn't actually bounced off those towering black sides?

With hand to mouth, Mr. Hunter called up, "Are her colors red, Mr. Adams? Does she fly the red flag! Is it the *Red Queen*?"

The *Red Queen* was Jack Steele's huge warship. Was the monster firing its cannons before us the flagship of that pirate king? Were we going to meet face to face with him at last? The great guns boomed again, and the burning sloop began to go down.

"Use your eyes!" Uncle Patch snapped. "The *Queen*'s the color of fresh blood, but that thing's the color of old pitch!" The strange ship fired again, a shattering broadside that sent up a storm of smoke. "Devil's heart, how many guns does the beast bear?"

Then the dawning light hit the great ship's flag. It was indeed red. And gold.

7

"She's a Spaniard, Captain!" sang out Mr. Adams. "Spanish flag as big as Castille and gaudy as a Mexican sunset!"

Hunter had seen as well, and his shoulders sagged. I knew he had been hoping for the *Red Queen* and for Jack Steele, for he bore the man an ancient grudge. But none of his disappointment showed in his voice as he called up, "And her adversaries, Mr. Adams?"

In the maintop, Mr. Adams clapped his telescope to his eye. "Can't tell anything of the sinking ones, sir, but the one that's left flies the Jolly Roger."

"Good," Uncle Patch said with a grim nod. "So the Dons are doing our job for us. More power to them, say I. Let's be off, now, and out of danger."

I stared at the massive ship as it loosed another broadside. I had never seen a Spanish warship before. She was long, broad, and tall, and gunfire erupted from at least three different decks. And she seemed strangely steady, barely rocking as the cannons fired.

"A real Spanish beauty, that one," said Mr. Jeffers, the one-eyed gunner next to me as he prepared his gun. He turned his head and gave me a grim smile.

"Slow as Christmas in stays, but she sails as steady as a castle on a rock. The Dons build them wide and heavy, they do. Not all slim and frenchified like this here skiff." Like most gunners, Mr. Jeffers felt that the whole aim of shipbuilding was to keep the guns steady.

"We have the wind gage. Bring her about, Mr. Warburton," Captain Hunter shouted to our hulking helmsman. "Stand ready for battle, men!"

"Ready for—have you lost your senses, man?" sputtered Uncle Patch, waving his arms. "She's a hundred forty feet stem to stern if an inch, she's probably got twice as many guns as we have, and she's so broad, you could berth the *Aurora* on her decks and not touch the rails! And she's sinking pirates! Pirates, for all love, and doing our very job for us! Leave the brute alone, William!"

Hunter grinned at him. "What, and miss this golden opportunity?"

My uncle glared at him. "You consider being blasted into waterlogged kindling a golden opportunity?"

Hunter stared across the sea at the ships. We were coming down with the wind, skimming fast toward them, and they grew moment by moment. Shaking his head, he said, "Why, you Irish leech, what better way to spread the legend of the daring pirate ship *Aurora* amongst the Brotherhood of the Coast than to save a shipload of buccaneers from the king of Spain?"

My uncle spluttered speechlessly.

"The captain's clapped a stopper on Patch," Mr. Jeffers guffawed, digging his horny elbow into my side. "He's got brains, he has. Ain't seen thinkin' that twisted since ol' Cap'n Morgan's day. 'Course, Cap'n Morgan couldn't sail worth a tinker's—"

I was no longer listening to Mr. Jeffers. I was trying to make myself as small as possible next to the railing. We were going into battle and I wanted to see it. As I wrote, we had taken our share of prizes in the previous months. But they had surrendered after a shot across their bows. None of them had carried anything like treasure, but Hunter had taken from them what booty they offered. After he had stripped the ships of powder and shot, he let them go, knowing they'd tell others that the *Aurora* was seeking prey.

This fight was going to be the real thing, and if

my uncle remembered he'd sent me onto the deck, I'd be back in the relative security of the surgery when the battle started, safe and blind as a doorknob. I fleetingly wondered where we were exactly. Two days before we had passed Puerto Rico on our larboard, and we had sailed mostly north and west since then, but I was no navigator. We were at sea, and that was all I knew.

Despite my uncle's logical ravings, the *Aurora,* once she had changed her tack, came down at a fine pace toward the battle. Mr. Adams, at a nod from Captain Hunter, ran up our own colors, a jet-black silk flag with a stark white skull and crossbones in the center. The crew had stopped laughing and shouting and instead stood crouched over their weapons and guns. Their faces were split into tight grins that reminded me of wolves. Or sharks.

In less time than it takes to tell, we were bearing down on the conflict. The Spaniard was between the burning sloop and her final enemy, off her starboard bow and maneuvering desperately to avoid the big ship's deadly broadside fire. We were coming up on the Spaniard's larboard stern, and so far she gave no sign of having spotted us.

"Aim for her masts and sheets, lads," Hunter shouted. "We don't have time to hammer her hull, and if we did, it would make no odds. I think she might just slap our faces for us. Cut her masts down! Once we're past her, we don't want her catching us! Hit her fast, hit her hard, and then run like the devil!"

We bore down on them, and the stern of the Spaniard loomed up. I saw running men at the rail. The Dons had spotted us, and they were fast to catch on that we weren't friends. Her two stern chasers opened up on us, but their shot went a hundred yards wide. Her best gunners must have been concentrating on her victims.

"A shame, I calls it," muttered Mr. Jeffers. "Best guns in the world and couldn't hit the broad side of Jamaica if they was anchored in Port Royal Harbor."

Then we were slipping by her and I could make out her name in huge gold letters across her stern: CONCEPCIÓN. I stared up great black wooden walls, my eyes wide. The *Concepción* towered at least ten to fifteen feet above us, like a castle on a rock.

"Fire as they bear!" ordered Mr. Hunter.

"Now's butcher's work, lad," Mr. Jeffers said with a grin, his slow-burning match steady over his gun's touchhole. "Up a mite. A mite more. Hold!" The gun crew had raised the barrel by wedging in quoins. They leaped away. I hunched behind the railing and stuffed my fingers in my ears. Then everything happened at once.

Mr. Jeffers whipped down his match and arched his body. His gun roared, recoiling with a devil's hammer blow that would have crushed any sailor behind it. As the smoke cleared, I saw the *Concepción*'s gunports fly open, exposing row upon row of gigantic twenty-four-pounders. The world erupted into ear-shattering sound and disappeared into a sulfuric cloud of gun smoke. The *Aurora* shuddered as the twenty-four-pound cannonballs screamed overhead and some slammed into us. I heard men screaming and cursing and stared in horror at the six-inch wooden splinter that quivered in the railing next to my head.

"Again, lads, again!" Hunter's bellow sounded far off and tiny after the gunfire. "Hit her again, before she can recover and hole us like cheese!"

Jeffers's crew had wormed and sponged the

cannon. Now they shoved in a cartridge of powder and a ball. Jeffers was already sighting. In shock I noticed that one of his ears was torn to a rag, blood streaming down his neck. I don't think he was even aware of it. "Steady! Steady!" he bawled, then with clenched teeth he rammed the slow-burning match fuse to the touchhole.

Then the *Aurora*'s cannons boomed again, and half-deafened though I was, I heard a crack like the gates of heaven falling. Through the billowing smoke I saw the Spaniard's mizzenmast go crashing down off to starboard. A wild cheer erupted from our crew, and Mr. Jeffers grinned through the blood on his face. "They're better armed, but we're better aimed, eh, lad?"

"Aye," I said, having read his lips to get his meaning. My head still rang with the crash of cannons. Now smoke was coming from the big Spaniard's deck, where the fallen sails had taken fire from their own cannon. I had a glimpse of the Spanish crew feverishly trying to prepare their guns for another round, but it was clear they were much slower than our own crews. They would not have time.

Then we cut right in front of the *Concepción*'s towering bluff bow, decorated with the figurehead of a woman with flowing blue robes. Spanish marines were firing their muskets at us and screaming what I could only assume were curses. I hazarded a quick look forward. The ship's forecastle had been hammered, its decking a shambles of twisted, splintered boards. One cannon had overturned, and the crew had wedged it, preventing it from sliding across the deck, through a hatch, and so through the bottom of the ship.

But the towering foremast was whole, its sails drawing. We pulled away from the crippled monster. Behind us, the *Concepción* struggled to turn, but it was clear that she could not do so in time to fire effectively. "Got her rudder, we did," yelled Abel Tate, one of our navy gunners, from astern. "Knocked it clean from its pintles!"

Another shout rang out, this time off to our starboard side. The remaining pirate sloop was desperately trying to put us between her and the *Concepción*. Captain Hunter was yelling orders that I, with my ringing ears, could scarcely follow, but the *Aurora* heeled as we adjusted our tack, sailing almost with the wind away from the Spaniard. She tried another broadside, but the shot merely ripped up the water astern of us.

We were going to get away. We had met a much superior foe, bloodied his nose, stolen his prize, and stolen ourselves from his angry jaws. I felt like shouting myself, but then I looked around.

The deck of the *Aurora* was littered with debris: splintered wood, bits of rope and rigging, and men—some bleeding and screaming, a few utterly still.

As we sailed away from the dawn and the crippled Spaniard raging behind us, I pulled myself together and ran to where I was needed. Uncle Patch was in the sick berth, stitching up a six-inch gash in old Ben Pond's arm. Ben, a gray-haired veteran with no teeth, watched the needle with interest and did not even flinch as it passed through his flesh. He gave me a friendly nod. "More comin'?" he asked.

"Aye," I said. "Half a dozen wounded above."

"Then I will need your help," my uncle said in an even tone of voice that told me I would be in trouble later for not being at his side earlier.

"Well," Ben said as Uncle Patch tied off and

snipped the catgut, "any gate, we touched up the big Spaniard and got away again."

As I helped him down and gave him the tot of rum that all the wounded could claim, I knew he was right. We had survived our first real battle. But the enemy had not let us get away unscathed.

Nor did I think he would forget us.

CHAPTER TWO

Captain Barrel

ALL THE REST OF that day we flew to the south and the west. When my uncle had finished his work, we found the butcher's bill, as Captain Hunter called it, was tolerable: seven wounds in all, none of them fatal, and only two dangerous. A foretopman named Leach had been hit by a musket ball that had lodged deep in his chest, pressing on the lung. My uncle took it out, bandaged him, and put him in the sick berth, where he lay gasping for breath. The other was a bad splinter wound, suffered by a swabber named Wilson on the forecastle. It called for a world of stitching, and still, the unfortunate man might lose the use of his right eye and perhaps of his arm.

When we were able to come on deck again, it was early afternoon, with a high tropical sun beating down. The ocean was as blue as ever I had seen it. Behind us the *Concepción* was nowhere to be seen, just the triangular sail of a very small vessel. Men were laboring at the pumps, sending jets of dirty gray water overboard, and forward, Captain Hunter was deep in consultation with the lean, scarred ship's carpenter, whom everyone called "Chips."

"I can't get at 'un," Chips was telling the captain earnestly. "We can fother 'un, but to plug 'un proper-like, we shall have to careen the barky, and where are we to do that?"

"A hole?" asked my uncle.

Hunter turned and stared at him, head to toe and up again. "You're all over blood, Patch."

"'Twas not I that spilled it," returned my uncle with a touch of impatience. "Come, tell me, are we sinking? For I have two sick men to think about."

"We be not sinkin', your honor," Chips protested in a hurt voice. "But we be hulled beneath the water-line for certain, an' takin' on more water than I like."

"Fother the hole," Hunter ordered. "We'll stand

in for Tortuga. Mr. Adams, we'll fly no colors. And while we're making our preparations, we'll let that pinnace come up. I have no doubt it holds the survivors from at least one of the sloops."

"And where's the other?" I asked. "The one that got away with us?"

"Two miles to larboard, off the bow," replied Hunter, and when I looked forward, I saw her there, a trim, single-masted sloop keeping easy pace with us.

"How about the men?" Hunter asked. "Any dead?"

"None, and sure, that's a wonder in itself," my uncle snapped. "Are we to do this always, I wonder? Go charging in where a well-placed broadside could send us to the bottom? Would it not be better to scuttle the ship at once, if that's your mind?"

Hunter shook his head, smiling. He cocked an eye at me. "You look downhearted, Davy. What's troubling you?"

I hardly wanted to say, because it would just make my uncle that much more angry, but at last I blurted out, "Why did we have to run from the Spaniard? We did more damage to her than she did to us!"

"A fire-eater!" Mr. Hunter said. Then, in a more serious tone, he added, "There's some truth in what your uncle says, Davy. The *Concepción* has twice our crew, maybe five hundred men all told. She mounts forty-eight cannons, all of them twenty-four-pounders, besides her swivel guns and chasers. And her scantlings are twice or three times as thick as ours. She could punch a hole in the *Aurora* as easy as I could kiss my hand, but our cannonballs would bounce right off her sides. Our only chance was to disable her and run, if we were to fight at all. Our men have big hearts, but they couldn't take a ship whose crew outnumbers us two or three to one."

"Still, we gave them a good fight," I said.

Hunter nodded. "That we did. And with any luck, word of that fight will get abroad. I hope that Jack Steele will hear it. He's up to some devilry, you may be sure, for he's been lying unnaturally low these last months. Whatever he's planning, I hope we can come to grips with him before his plot has hatched."

I watched as the men prepared to fother the hole. That meant, as I saw, that they used an old sail. They lowered it from the bows with ropes and worked it back along the hull until they had it over the unseen hole, then made it fast. Soon Chips reported that we were taking on water at a slower rate. We'd still have to pump our way into port, but at least we would not sink.

The time that the temporary repair took gave the little craft behind us the chance to catch up. Nineteen men crowded it, and our crew helped them aboard. Most of the newcomers were wounded, and my uncle met them as they came one by one to our deck. "You'll wait," he said to one. "I know a broken arm hurts like the very devil, but your shipmates are bleeding. This man's dead. I'll take you first," he said to a pale man whose shipmates had lashed his chest with sailcloth through which blood seeped.

Back we went to the sick berth, where the unlucky devil died before my uncle could do anything more than examine his chest wound. "Next," he said, turning from the corpse. Of the nineteen men in the little craft, two were dead, including the chest wound, and eleven more were injured. We took off one unfortunate man's leg at the knee, he screaming through the operation and passing out at last. Our final patient had merely a burn along his arm and a few deep cuts that took some stitches. "And what vessel were you from, lad?" my uncle asked as he plied his needle.

The young sailor, not more than four years older than I was—say sixteen or so—was weeping from pain. "We were o' the *Vengeance*," he said in a weak voice. "Though we picked up three men from the *Tally*, what sunk before we did."

"Gentlemen of fortune, I take it?" observed my uncle, tying off his catgut. "Come, lad, you can tell me, for we sail on account ourselves."

"Aye," groaned the young man. "Cap'n Pearse was the master, an' we'd joined with the *Tally* an' the *Fury* to stand against that Spanish devil."

"The *Concepción*. A Spanish naval vessel, is she?"

The injured man shook his head. "No, not at all. They say her captain is Don Esteban de Reyes. She's a pirate hunter, she is, and a private ship."

"Oh, so?" my uncle asked in evident surprise. "A dear expense she must be! I make no doubt that this Don Esteban is a rich man. Davy, a tot for our patient."

When we had finished our second round of

operating, we went back onto the deck. The two dead sailors had been sewn up into hammocks, with a round shot sewn in at their feet. Captain Hunter read the burial service over them, and our men tipped them over the side, to sink into the ocean. One of the few uninjured sailors from the *Vengeance* muttered a gruff thanks. "Not many of us gets a real funeral," he said. "'Tis a mort o' comfort to see our shipmates bein' given a proper send-off."

It was nearly sunset, and the remaining sloop, the *Fury*, had hauled much closer in. She was now only a few hundred yards away, and as he turned from the burial service, Captain Hunter shook his head once more at my uncle's appearance. "You'll have to wash and change clothes," he said. "For the captain of that sloop is coming aboard to dine with us, and you're far too bloody for company."

Uncle Patch waved his fingers irritably. "Tiddle-diddle! You're far too delicate in your tastes for a pirate. But as my sleeves are somewhat stiff, I shall do as you say. However, I'm here to tell you that all the wounded we took aboard will live to be hanged yet. Now, what you are going to do with them—"

"I propose to let the captain of the sloop take them," Hunter replied. "But do make ready. I hope you are hungry."

"Faith, my innards are wolves," my uncle told him. "For I've had neither bite nor sup this day, so busy have you kept me."

We went below, and soon enough we had washed up and changed clothing. My uncle even shaved, something he sometimes neglected to do for days on end, so that normally his cheeks bristled with copper-red whiskers. When we were clean and decent, we joined Captain Hunter in his cabin at the stern of the ship. A huge man sat in an armchair, a man with a wooden leg thrust straight out before him. His hair was dark, long, and tangled, and his beard fell to his waist. He wore a single silver-buckled shoe, ragged canvas trousers, no shirt, and a stained blue jacket. Around his neck was a necklace of shark's teeth.

"My surgeon, Dr. Patch," Mr. Hunter said as we came in. "And his loblolly boy and nephew, Davy Shea. Gentlemen, this is Captain John Barrel, of the sloop *Fury*."

Captain Barrel nodded in a companionable way.

"Aye, and a grateful man this day," he rumbled with a flashing white grin. "But for your gunners, me an' my crew would be feedin' the fishes now, so we would. Curse that Spaniard! He come at us from the dark, and before we knew it, we were fightin' for our lives. Cap'n Tucker o' the *Tally* struck his colors, so he did, an' that Spanish devil fired into his sinking craft nonetheless. No quarter give, none asked."

The cook knocked respectfully and said, "Vittles is up."

"Draw your chair to the table, Captain Barrel," Hunter said. "Our fare is rough, but there's plenty."

"Thunder, but you do yourselves right," Barrel observed as the cook's men brought in hot soup, ship's bread, and wine. "Aboard o' my craft, the sailors wouldn't put up with this. We eats together, we does."

"Your host was once an officer in the Royal Navy," Uncle Patch said, pouring wine for Barrel. "And the men like to keep up navy ways."

"Some of 'em ain't so bad," replied Barrel. He took a deep drink of wine. "Ahhhh! Now, that's seen the right bottle, that has."

As we ate, Barrel told us about his own crew.

They had elected him captain, in the way of pirates, and they were a stouthearted bunch. He was shorthanded, though, and he readily agreed to take on the remaining crew of the sunken *Tally* and *Vengeance*, saying that the wounds made no matter. "I can use any man what can stand and haul on a line," he declared. "Though I ain't seein' any fightin' for the next few days. We're precious short o' provisions, an' I mean to put into Tortuga."

"That's where we're bound," Captain Hunter said. "We need careening. Tell me, is it still wide open?"

Sorrowfully, Barrel shook his head. "Not as it was when I was a younker. The French signed a blasted treaty with the Spaniards three or four years agone, so a man can't just haul in with the Jolly Roger a-flyin'. Still, nobody there bothers ye much if ye don't go roarin' up the middle o' the street. 'Tis safe enough, I reckon. They still don't love the Spanish, an' the port admiral, a man named du Pont, will do right by ye, so long as ye grease him with a little gold."

By the end of the meal, Barrel had agreed to sail in consort with us, at least as far as Tortuga, three days' sail away, if the wind held true. It was evening by the time he stumped back onto deck. He caught me looking at his wooden leg and clapped me on the shoulder. "That there timber toe o' mine," he said, "I got when the *Thunderer* went down off the coast o' Madagascar. I was goin' ashore clingin' to a grate, for I can't swim a lick, when a almighty big shark took a bite o' me. I had my knife, so I fought back, in course, but he got the best o' the bargain, for he took my leg." He rattled the necklace he wore. "All I got was his teeth!"

Some of our men had agreed to row Barrel over to his sloop, and I went along. As we rowed, Barrel lowered his voice and asked, "Now, lad, tell me: Is what they say about Hunter true? Did he blow up half o' Fort Morgan an' kill a dozen British soldiers when he got away from Port Royal?"

"At least a dozen," I said, lying my head off, for we had killed no one in that farce. "Hunter was a mutineer, you know. He has the death sentence on him, and so does my uncle."

"Aye, so I heard," said Barrel thoughtfully. "So has he taken any prizes?"

"Many of them," I said. "British and Spanish, but no French so far."

"Good, for though Tortuga ain't what it was, no, not by a long chalk, the French ain't bad if you don't bother them. Thank ye, matey. Ye ease my mind, that ye do."

When we had delivered the one-legged captain and I was alone with my uncle again, I told him of Barrel's questions and about the lies I had told.

"I feel bad about it," I finished. "He's a rough man, but he seemed so grateful."

Uncle Patch was in his hammock, his spectacles on his nose, reading a book on medicine. He closed it and nodded. "He's a brave man, no doubt of it, and with some conscience for his sailors, which is not always the case. But a man can be likable and still be a scoundrel, Davy. It doesn't seem fair, but there it is. Now get to your berth, for we have lessons tomorrow."

I groaned. We always had lessons.

But the next morning, as we sat down in the cabin with my books, I had a surprise. Mr. Adams was there. He explained in a shy, halting voice, that Captain Hunter thought him capable of learning mathematics and passing his examination for lieutenant, his life's desire. "It's true I have a thick head when it comes to figures," he said. "I'm willing to try, though, if you will have me."

My uncle raised no objection, and I was glad to have company in my misery. That morning we were beginning the rudiments of trigonometry. Surely there never was a more unfitted teacher for this than my uncle, whose grasp of mathematics ended at the five times table. But he was never less than willing.

He opened a book and cleared his throat. "Now, then. Pythagoras. Pythagoras was an ancient Greek, and as everyone knows, he was the learned man of the world when it came to triangles. So, so. Pythagoras tells us of a wonderful feature of a right triangle—right meaning your true, your correct triangle, I take it. A triangle has, let us see, three angles, which the name tells us plainly enough, and each angle is made up of two sides, and therefore a triangle has six sides—no, no, I'm out, for the sides do double duty, to be sure—"

After a bit, Mr. Adams, with a deep frown of concentration, suggested that perhaps a right triangle contained one right angle, one angle of ninety degrees, a fact that he knew from the way noon sights were taken. My uncle agreed. We worked our way around to the hypotenuse, not the river creature of Africa, as Uncle Patch explained, but rather the side that sat across the room from that right angle.

It took much explaining and not a little backtracking and consulting the book, but finally Mr. Adams nodded, surprise on every feature. "So," he said, "if we multiply the length of the hypotenuse by itself, that number then is equal to the sums of the squares of the other two sides of the triangle! And is this true for all right triangles, no matter how big?"

"It is," my uncle said, closing the book. "And that is why Pythagoras was such a deep old file, may God set a flower on his head. And so we turn to Latin—"

Mr. Adams left us then, for he was only in it for the mathematics. But I shall never forget the light in his face. He had made his first step toward being a lieutenant, and somehow I felt then that he would not stop until he had reached his goal.

CHAPTER THREE

Pirates' Den

FOR DAYS WE LIMPED toward the island of Tortuga, just north of the bigger island called Hispaniola. Even with the leak plugged, the men pumped for hours every day. In the cabin one morning, as Captain Hunter was writing up the ship's log from hasty scribbled notes, I asked him and my uncle what the islands were like.

In answer, Captain Hunter crumpled a piece of paper into a wad and tossed it onto the table. "Like that," he said. "Rugged and broken and mountainous."

"And of old a haunt of pirates," added my uncle.

So on the morning that the lookout in the

maintop called down, "Land ho!" I was prepared for what I saw: a dark, humped island on the horizon, looking very much like that wad of crumpled paper.

"Trim the sails, lads," Captain Hunter called out. "Make her look sweet and innocent."

"As innocent as a battered Frenchman with twenty-eight guns can look," Uncle Patch muttered under his breath.

Hunter turned to him with a grin. "It's all in the attitude, Patch! Where's your sense of adventure, man?"

"I left it behind in Dublin, where I should be as well!" snapped my uncle with a glower.

The *Fury* was far ahead as we sailed eastward along the rugged northern coast of Hispaniola. Finally, the morning after our landfall, we sailed straight into the open arms of Tortuga Harbor, bold as brass and twice as bright.

We followed a pilot boat through one of the two channels that led into the harbor. I could see batteries of cannons on either side of the headlands and the great fort on its hill over the town, in turn dwarfed by a more distant mountain that towered above it. The fort looked sullen and old and humorless. The sunlight barely illuminated its guns, black and hidden within the shadows of the fort's walls. I felt they were staring at me. The town itself, called Cayona, was a ramshackle collection of stone houses and driftwood huts, the waterfront thronging with jostling crowds.

"Looking for real pirates, Davy?" Uncle Patch rumbled with disapproval behind me. "Just keep an eye peeled, and you'll see 'em all around you."

The harbor was thick with ships and boats of all shapes and sizes. Many were small sloops and brigs, clustered around the wharves and piers, but some were larger, including two merchantmen whose shabby sides were rough with peeling paint. One, at least, was well armed, for she had new gunports cut into her old sides.

"Pirate ships?" I asked, and my uncle nodded. "How can you tell?"

Shaking his head so that his red ponytail swayed, Uncle Patch replied, "Saints, it would be easier to tell which ones aren't, for there are not so many of them. Not so many years ago, Tortuga was wide open. The place made Port Royal look like a monastery. Then the French and the Dons signed a treaty saying piracy was a bad thing. And all the blessed piece of paper did was make the pirates less obvious. You can still buy anything and sell anything, no matter how crookedly come by, so long as you don't ask or answer questions about the goods."

By noon, the *Aurora* was tied fast to one of the wharves, the *Fury* penned in front of us. Captain Barrel stamped around her deck, lashing out with his fist and delivering kicks with his wooden leg to encourage his crew. Then he stood on the *Fury*'s stern and grinned up at us.

"Ahoy, Cap'n Hunter!"

"Ahoy yourself, Captain Barrel!" Captain Hunter called back. "Here we all are, living proof that the good Lord has a love for scoundrels."

Barrel roared with laughter. "Aye! And at least we're honest enough as scoundrels go. If ye wants to see a son o' Satan, though, just cast an eye to larboard!"

Our eyes followed his pointing hand. A galley, a vessel about the size of a sloop and equipped with long oars, was making its way across the harbor toward us. She was crusted with gilt, and I saw a huge French flag snapping from her single mast.

Barrel called out, "I've sent a man in to say a good word for you, so p'rhaps Monsieur du Pont will leave you your small clothes!" He gurgled with laughter, then wiped his eyes and looked more serious. "Aye, for piracy you need nerve, but for real thieving you need a port official!"

"Wonderful," muttered Hunter, staring as the oarsmen moved the galley toward us. "Whoever Monsieur du Pont may be, Captain Barrel's description doesn't bode well."

My uncle shook his head. "William, no port official bodes well. That must be the man himself standing in the prow. Smile for the greedy son of a rum-puncheon!" And so we did, myself included, as the galley came alongside and the port admiral of Tortuga hauled himself onboard.

"Captain Hunter," the man said, spreading his mouth in a smile and looking around. "Permit me to introduce myself. I am Charles du Pont, at your service." From where I stood behind my uncle, I thought that M. Charles du Pont had an uncanny resemblance to a toad. He was short, with a flabby, round body, and had a wide, lipless mouth and bulging eyes. There was an oily slickness to him that all the embroidery and lace in the world could not hide.

With him was a harassed-looking little man armed with a heavy ledger and a bedraggled quill pen. His murmuring voice droned behind the port admiral like a mayfly's buzz: "Harbor fee . . . wharf fee . . . cordage tax . . . water shipage . . . careenage . . . victualing fee . . ."

Ignoring him, Captain Hunter bowed politely, a fixed grin on his face. "Monsieur du Pont, we are in your hands. I'm Captain William Hunter. Welcome aboard the *Aurora*."

The bulging eyes swiveled in the fat, round face. The man seemed incapable of blinking. He inclined his head a bit on his heavy neck and said, "Alas, you arrive at a most inopportune time, Captain Hunter. Tortuga is very crowded." He waved a hand at the harbor, his thick fingers wiggling like sausages on a toasting fork. "You see the way the ships are packed in. Repairs may be"—he waggled those fingers—"unfortunately slow."

Captain Hunter's smile had become so fixed, it

looked nailed on. "Well, that's bad for us. We hit a . . . reef and stove in our bow below the waterline. We badly need to careen the ship to get at the leak."

"A reef?" M. du Pont's blank gaze swiveled to our forecastle. Despite everything Chips had been able to do, it still showed damage from cannon fire. "Yes. Reefs can be most treacherous."

"We'll need new planking," Captain Hunter said. "And I'm sure we'll have to recopper some of the hull."

My uncle added, "And I need to buy medicines. To my shame, my medical chest is almost empty."

The bulging toad eyes swung back at us. I felt like a bug. Slowly, the port admiral's pudgy right hand came up, and his clerk's buzzing drone—"lumber . . . new copper . . ."—trailed off into silence.

Looking my uncle up and down, but speaking to Hunter, du Pont said, "I take it this is your ship's doctor?"

"Alas, for my poor manners!" Hunter bowed again, as elegantly as he might have done before King James himself. "Monsieur du Pont, I beg to present to you Dr. Patrick Shea, ship's surgeon of the *Aurora*."

The lipless mouth smiled, which made Uncle Patch scowl even more. "So many ships that put in here have no surgeon at all. And are you well schooled as a surgeon, Monsieur Shea?"

"Tolerably well," said my uncle. "I took my training at Trinity College in Dublin."

"Impressive. It is not often that a real doctor visits our outpost." The port admiral's smile grew wider, until it looked as if it were going to touch his ears. "Let us have a talk, Captain. I think I see in your physician here a solution to problems, both mine and yours."

The two men walked away, almost arm in arm, followed by the now silent clerk and his ledger, leaving Uncle Patch and me standing alone on the deck.

"There he goes," muttered my uncle sourly. "And, by all that's holy, 'twill be lucky for us if the smooth-talking Monsieur du Pont leaves us with a plank for our ship and a rag for a sail!"

Three hours after the captain and du Pont had their talk, my uncle and I were in a carriage rolling through the rutted streets of Cayona, my uncle cursing at each jolt of the wheels. "That misbe-gotten—never trust an Englishman, Davy!" he snarled.

"'Twas a fair bargain, you know," I told him.

"I know nothing of the sort!" he returned.

I sighed heavily and leaned back into the cracked leather. Uncle Patch would rail against Captain Hunter until his voice gave out.

But I was remembering what M. du Pont had said to Mr. Hunter: "The expenses could be lower, Captain Hunter. Call it a favor for a favor. A rich man here in town, Monsieur Gille, a good friend of the governor, has a . . . special guest. Like your vessel, this guest has suffered an accident, has run upon a reef, so to speak. His life is despaired of, but if your ship's surgeon can save him, then I believe I can guarantee speedy repairs and fair prices."

So Captain Hunter had made his bargain: Uncle Patch would treat this mysterious guest, and we wouldn't have to sell the *Aurora* to pay her port fees. My uncle's surgical kit was wedged between us and bounced back and forth, slamming our shins as we jounced from rut to rut. The streets were terrible, but the French only shrugged their shoulders.

Le bon Dieu, they said, had ruined the streets with bad weather, and *le bon Dieu* could repair them, for no one else would.

Cayona was a strange mix of substantial stone and tabby buildings and haphazard wooden shacks and canvas tents. Everywhere I heard French being bellowed, being shrieked, being flung upon the sultry air in what might have been jokes or curses, for all I knew. We left the town behind and rumbled up a twisting road between trees whose roots spread out over what looked like solid rock.

Indeed, what it was that M. Gille grew on that stony ground I could not guess. The plantation house the carriage driver took us to was a stone affair, square and two-storied, with a red tile roof. To reach it, we had to pass through a barred iron gate in a tall stone wall. A silent servant opened it for us and closed it behind with a clang.

Uncle Patch muttered, "Saints, but that bears a frosty sound, like the clapping to of a cell door!" Ahead, down a long lane lined with palm trees, stood the house. It had been whitewashed recently, and it fairly shone in the light of the afternoon sun.

A purple-liveried servant met us at the door and

silently gestured for us to follow. The driver walked behind us with the surgical kit. Our footsteps echoed on the cool tiles until we reached a low, dark room. I thought we were alone until a man emerged from the shadows.

He was tall and slim and as pale a man as I had ever seen. The long white wig he wore made his face look even more bloodless. His suit was neat and well tailored but brown as cured tobacco and just as drab. His voice, however, was soft and smooth, like honey strained through silk, and it was an English voice, not a French one: "Good day to you, Dr. Shea. I am Robert Meade, Monsieur Gille's estate manager. My employer sends his regrets but he is unable to attend to you personally. He hopes you understand."

"Perfectly," snapped my uncle. "He's a grandee and doesn't want to spot his hands with the blood of this poor wretch I'm to treat."

Mr. Meade smiled a wintry smile. "It is good that we understand each other. Cesar will remain here. Your boy may carry your instruments. This way, if you please."

I didn't see him move, but suddenly a section of

wood paneling behind him slipped aside, revealing a dark room barely lit by candlelight. I took the case from the driver, and for the first time noticed that he wore a cutlass at his side. He stood with one hand on the hilt, as if he had changed from servant to guard.

The hidden room was lit only by a single candle and one high, very narrow slit of window. There was a table, two chairs, and a long bed with a straw mattress. A man lay on this, moaning softly.

Mr. Meade raised a hand to hold my uncle back. "A word first. You will speak to no one of your patient. You will treat him, doing whatever you feel necessary, and then you will report to me. Should you need any assistance, please inform Cesar." He dropped his hand and walked out with a strange elegance that totally belied his dull attire.

Uncle Patch went straight to the feverishly thrashing figure on the bed. The man was muttering in a voice that seemed oddly familiar to me, though what he said had no sense in it: "Steady as she goes, Mr. Twinings . . . bring her about, bring her about!"

Uncle Patch snatched the candlestick from its

table and held it up. "Saints in heaven!" he said, with a sharp intake of breath.

In the candlelight I recognized the drawn face, flushed with fever beneath a bloody bandage around the head. It was familiar, but horribly changed, all sharp cheekbones and sagging skin. Empty eyes stared up at nothing, blank and blue as a West Indies sky. Captain Brixton? Could this wasted wax figure actually be the robust captain of the *Retribution*? The last time I had seen him he had been yelling curses at us as the *Swift* had fled from Port Royal. Captain Brixton was the only man, other than Sir Henry Morgan and King James himself, who knew we weren't really pirates.

He groaned and flung a hand over his eyes, still muttering as if giving commands: "Solid shot, Mr. Bellows . . . stand by, stand by . . . she's firing on us!"

Uncle Patch was moving methodically down the wasted body, checking and probing. "Instruments, Davy. He's on fire with fever. I'll need cold water, clean rags. And light! Tell them I need lanterns, candles, whatever they have!"

I sprinted to the door and blurted out Uncle Patch's demands to Cesar. He nodded, went to the outer door, and called in French. Before long, a silent servant brought in a bucket of cool well water and a bundle of clean rags. A second trip brought enough candles to light a cathedral.

For what seemed like forever, I sponged the captain's face and chest as we fought to bring his fever down. Uncle Patch poured various potions down his throat, shaking his head and muttering under his breath almost as loudly as the captain himself. His long fingers removed the bandage, and my uncle swore at what he saw. High on Captain Brixton's left forehead was a depressed place, purple and ugly. My uncle muttered, "Davy, we have to go into this man's skull. I hope you have the stomach for it."

First, though, he ordered the strangest thing I had heard yet: for a silver piece to be hammered thin. When Cesar brought one in, he tested it, found it unsatisfactory, and had it rehammered until it was a slightly rounded little dome. He nodded at that.

And though I had seen terrible wounds, I was hardly prepared for this. Under the glare of candles, we lashed the captain to the bed. Then my uncle cut skin and flesh away, folding it back as I held the captain's head steady with one arm wrapped around and my hand pressed beneath his chin. With my free hand, I swabbed blood. My uncle used a curious circular silver saw to cut away a disk of bone. I gasped as he lifted this away and a gush of fluid came forth, with a dark clot of blood at its center. Beneath that, pink and throbbing, lay Captain Brixton's brain.

Working quickly, my uncle fastened the silver dome to the skull with wonderfully tiny screws from his case, and then he stitched the scalp back. At last we untied our patient, and as soon as we were done, Uncle Patch patted my shoulder. "You'll be a fine surgeon one day," he said gruffly. Weary and sick though I felt, I assure you that kind word made me stand a bit taller.

Captain Brixton lay easier, apparently deep asleep. My uncle was even more wrinkled than usual, his good black suit crusted with blood. His eyes were red-rimmed and swollen. He replaced his instruments in their case and strode to the open doorway, where Mr. Meade met us. "How is he?"

Uncle Patch walked right past him. "I need air."

Mr. Meade made some signal to Cesar, and then he followed us to the front door. Night had fallen, and my uncle stood on the veranda of the house taking great breaths. At last he turned to Mr. Meade. "The man is to have rest and quiet. Turn him gently every three hours so he will not be eaten up with bedsores. Change the dressing on the wound twice a day, and make sure the new one is clean."

Mr. Meade nodded. "It will be done."

My uncle puffed out his cheeks. "The man may be paralyzed down his right side, and probably blind in that eye. If he recovers, 'tis the Lord's work, not mine."

Mr. Meade summoned the carriage, and my uncle and I stepped into it for our trip back to the harbor. But not before Meade's long, slim fingers had slipped a small leather bag into my hand, with the weight and clink of gold.

In the cabin of the *Aurora*, Captain Hunter leaped from his seat when my uncle told him whom we had operated upon. "Brixton!" he thundered. "Is he in danger?"

"Mortal danger," my uncle shot back. "And if he

does live, by some mercy, he's a mere wreck for the rest of his life, a hulk stove in and on the rocks."

"What happened to him?" Hunter demanded.

"That I know not, for he's not in his right mind, at all," Uncle Patch said.

"I believe I do." We all spun round at the new voice. Mr. Adams stood in the doorway, his hat in hand. "Begging your pardon, Captain, but I've been going around town, listening, as you ordered. The *Retribution* got herself blown to glory off Santiago last week."

Hunter reached for his sword. "We have to rescue him."

My uncle seized his arm. "Whisht, you hotheaded Englishman, stop and think! How can you rescue a man you can't move? His life is tied to his body by threads. If you move him, you'll kill him sure!"

Captain Hunter gave him the coldest stare I have ever seen. "Are we to do nothing?" He waved his sword.

My uncle said impatiently, "Put that thing away, for I could not sew my own nose back on! We'll do what we can. Listen, now: In three days' time—four at most—I'll know whether he is to be moved or be buried. Either way, Captain Alexander Brixton's sailing days are over."

As I stood there, I wondered whether Captain Brixton would live. If he did, would he thank my uncle for saving him, or curse him?

For the choice between death and the kind of life he seemed doomed to have if he survived was a sorry choice indeed.

CHAPTER FOUR

The Grandee

THE SIDES OF TORTUGA Harbor were remarkably steep. The whole island rose from the sea like a tortoise's back, which, I learned, was how it got its name, for *tortuga* means "sea turtle" in Spanish. However, in one spot there was a fairly level careening ground, and to this Captain Hunter sailed the *Aurora*. It was partly with the help of the harbor crew, but mostly by our own efforts, that we careened the frigate.

That meant we first roused out of her hold everything she carried. Over several weary days, barrels and bags and crates had to be hauled ashore, where they were locked inside a warehouse.

Into a different storage house went cannons, shot, and powder. Hunter set two sailors to guard each door day and night, the hands taking watches of four hours a turn on guard duty. There was some mild complaining about this, for the men who had sailed with Sir Henry Morgan knew Tortuga well. To them, guarding the doors seemed like a man sitting in his own bed with a loaded pistol on his lap—at least until they noticed how the port had changed since the old days. Then the complaining ceased, and the lookouts kept a good watch.

Once the ship was empty, we hauled her sideways up wooden ramps and tilted her over, so that she lay on her starboard side. It took the whole crew, pulling with a will as they chanted a sea song, to do this, even with the help of blocks and tackles. The *Aurora* slid up on greased wooden skids, tilted over, and came to rest at last.

On the February day when we careened the ship, I remember how astonished I was at seeing the *Aurora*'s bottom. She wore a sheathing of copper sheets, but even so, the dripping, dark green weed grew thick and matted on her, like a long, shaggy beard. The hole showed up too, a punched-in crater more than a foot across. Chips clucked his tongue when he saw it. "'Tis a mercy that evil-hearted Spaniard hit us only once in such a place. Twice would've been right awkward, and three times would've sunk us."

That day the crew found quarters ashore, many of them in boardinghouses, but most in a kind of tent city thrown up in the spaces behind and between the warehouses, overlooking the careened ship. Abel Tate told me that it was needful to stay close to the frigate. "Lord a' mercy," he muttered, "but who would trust the barky to be safe with these here French thieves so thick on the ground?"

"You think they'd bother the ship?" I asked the short, wiry sailor.

He gave me a quick nod. "Lord love ye, they'd take the blessed hatch gratings themselves, so they would. Aye, and strip the gold paint from the figure-head!"

At first it was interesting to watch the men scrape the weed from the ship, shaving it off so that the copper shone through. But the smell was terrible, and glad I was when my uncle found us lodging in a kind of hotel overlooking the bay. It was a curious place, unlike The King's Mercy in Jamaica where we had lived. Its name was the Royale, but there was nothing royal about it.

The building was a stone pile of three stories, with a dark sort of public house on the ground floor and above that a warren of small rooms. Ours had a window with no glass in it, but shutters that we could close if so minded. My uncle took the bed, a wooden frame with a lumpy straw mattress, and I made do with the floor, which I think was probably the more comfortable of the two.

The owner was a sour, fat Frenchman with a protruding lower lip and a villainous squint. He spoke little, but was ever sharp to charge Uncle Patch for the least little thing: for his taking a glass of ale to the room, or for closing the shutters on a day of no rain.

Cayona reminded me of Port Royal, except that the town was louder and rougher. Stone buildings stood cheek by jowl next to ramshackle wooden ones that might have worn paint forty years earlier but that now stood bare to the sun and the weather. Everywhere was a gabble of French. The merchants and their customers seemed unable to conduct business at all unless it was at the very top of their lungs, with much arm-waving and scolding.

More men were in the streets than women, a good deal more. As Uncle Patch had said, in lots of ways Tortuga was still the pirates' nest it had been forty years before. 'Twas true the buccaneers no longer flew their Jolly Rogers, but tried to do business as if they were respectable sailors. Still, many and many a piratical-looking wretch did I see skulking though the busy streets.

M. du Pont proved quite congenial. Evidently M. Gille gave him a good account of my uncle's visit, and it took only a thumping great bribe from Mr. Hunter to make du Pont happy to help us. The toadlike port admiral often stopped to see how work on the frigate was coming. He thanked my uncle three or four times for his excellent treatment of the English prisoner. Uncle Patch accepted the thanks with what was, for him, a gracious air, though he had told no one except Mr. Hunter that the patient was Captain Brixton. Twice every week Uncle Patch went to check on Brixton's progress and to take him medicines, but never did he allow me to go with him.

Toward the end of the first week in February, M. du Pont waddled by just as Chips had chopped out the damaged planking and had begun to measure the wood he needed to replace it. Hunter stood in his working clothes, breeches and a plain gray shirt, watching as Chips crept over the hull. I was next to the captain when du Pont came to stand beside us, leaning on his cane. "A grievous great hole," he murmured in his accented English. "*Mon Dieu*, it is lucky that you did not strike twice upon such a reef."

"It is, at that," agreed Captain Hunter, though I thought that du Pont knew as well as we did that the "reef" that made the hole was a twenty-four-pound cannon. "However, the ship is sound. We hope to have her afloat in another week."

"*Bien*," du Pont said, his lipless smile splitting his face. He prodded at the gravel with his cane. "I have in fact come to extend to you an invitation, Captain. My good friend Monsieur Etienne Gille would be grateful if you would favor him with your presence at dinner tonight."

"I am very busy here," Hunter pointed out.

"*Oui*, the repair of the ship, it calls for attention,

certainly," agreed du Pont. He waved his fat right hand in the air delicately. "But my friend Monsieur Gille is, how do you say, an important man, a grandee, as the Spanish call them. Very wealthy, and he has a voice in the government of the island, too. He could be someone you . . . need to know."

"So?" asked Captain Hunter, with a quizzical tilt of his head. He appeared to think the matter over for a moment, and then nodded. "Very well. What time?"

"At seven in the evening. The plantation is not far from town. I will give you directions there—or your surgeon may accompany you. Monsieur Shea knows the way by now." M. du Pont smiled again, though the expression did not light his dark, bulging eyes at all. "Tortuga can still be a friendly place for a gentleman who knows his allies. I hope we both may benefit from your acquaintance with Monsieur Gille."

"Thank you," Captain Hunter said in a wry voice. "Now if you could find me a few square yards of copper sheeting, how happy I would be."

M. du Pont's smile widened, making him even more froglike. "Monsiuer, I am at your service. If you have the gold, voilà! Like an alchemist, I can change it to copper."

The port admiral had begun to stroll away, when Captain Hunter called after him: "I say! One question. Will it truly be acceptable for Doctor Shea to come along? I'm sure he would like to see his patient again. He tells me the poor devil was badly hurt."

M. du Pont spread his hands, grasping his walking stick as if he were a conjurer and it was his wand. "But of course! I may speak for Monsieur Gille when I say he would be delighted of Doctor Shea's presence. *Au revoir.*"

That evening all three of us set out, for I had talked my way into the party as a servant. It was a hot journey, even in early February, and as we toiled up the winding streets in our finery, my uncle constantly grumbled about his discomfort. "We might have taken a chaise," he pointed out. "Five miles of walking is no joke, not when the ground underfoot is this unyielding rock. It was rough enough in that blasted carriage."

"I think it's as well to get the lay of the land," Captain Hunter coolly replied. "Especially since we may need to bring Captain Brixton away suddenly."

My uncle shot him a dark look. "Faith, and if ye bring him away suddenly tonight, 'tis a corpse you'll bear. I tell you, 'tis still a toss-up whether he lives or dies. We'll be in port for another week or ten days, Mr. Adams says. Give Captain Brixton at least that long to mend before you play some hare-brained trick."

Hunter smiled sweetly, but he would not swear that he would abide by my uncle's advice, so Uncle Patch was in a foul mood by the time we had left the town behind and sighted once again the grim iron gates of the Gille plantation.

A servant wearing splendid purple satin livery showed us into a grandly furnished room where M. du Pont rose from a chair to make the introductions. M. Etienne Gille was a sleek and elegant man, who wore an elaborate curled black wig that fell to his shoulders, and a rich brocaded suit in maroons and purples. His face was round, smooth, and pale as an egg. He led us to the dining room, and as my uncle's servant, I took my place behind his chair when Gille urged his guests to be seated.

He whispered something to a servant, and the man scurried out. A few moments later, another man, taller than Gille and slim as a Spanish blade, joined us. He wore a luxuriant silvery white wig and modest snuff-colored clothing, but even had he changed, I would have recognized the mysterious Mr. Meade.

"Captain Hunter," said M. Gille in his smooth way, "permit me to introduce Monsieur Robert Meade, my business adviser. I believe he has always ready made the acquaintance of Doctor Shea?"

"Mr. Meade has been most helpful," my uncle said without much expression in his voice. The tall man smiled softly and bowed in acknowledgment.

Gille nodded amiably. "As you can see, Monsieur Meade is English, like yourselves, though his French is impeccable. I asked him to join us in case there are any little difficulties of language."

Meade again politely inclined his head but did not speak, and indeed from that moment he might almost have faded into the woodwork, so quiet did he remain. The meal was a rich one, with many courses, and it went on for more than two hours. My uncle asked if he might have a quick look at his patient, and M. Gille agreed, though he said, "Later, if you please, after our dinner."

For most of the time, the men's talk was of trivial matters—the weather, the state of shipping, the tension between Spain and England. Finally, though, M. Gille put both of his hands flat upon the table, cleared his throat, and said, "My good friend Monsieur du Pont thought it would be well for us to meet, my dear Captain, and I see that he was correct. Now what I have to say to you must remain confidential. We are men of the world. I am sure you understand."

"Men of the world, are we?" asked my uncle in so agreeable a voice that I knew he was ready to explode.

M. Gille apparently did not hear him. He rested his elbows on the arms of his chair and made a tent of his fingers. He tapped them together a few times and then said, "How to explain. My friend, as a merchant and as the adviser of the governor of Tortuga, I have many interests. Shipping is one of them. I do not actually own many vessels, but I concern myself with the welfare of many captains— many captains." He took a sip of wine. "How shall I put this? I am the—call it the friend, no, better, the sponsor—of many an enterprising captain, of many a willing crew."

M. du Pont had been drinking more wine than the others. He leaned forward with a foolish smile on his fat face. "My friend means that an, uh, independent captain needs protection. Needs a port open and amicable to him. Needs a, how do you say, a refuge at times."

"A place of safety," Hunter said with a smile. "A haven to fly to when the—weather turns bad."

M. du Pont laughed coarsely. "The weather! *Oui!* When the weather is, let us say, stormy! That is good."

Gille did not look at du Pont, but his right eye began to twitch. "Weather is one concern," he said in a dry voice.

M. du Pont cut him short: "Listen, my friends! With Monsieur Gille's help, you can make your fortunes! Tortuga will be always open to you, and you may sell your cargo, *any cargo*, at a handsome profit. He will arrange to have any vessels you do not need sold, for ready money, and for this he takes only a small percentage. There are heaps of gold to be made from goods taken from merchant ships—salvaged, we could say. Or ransom! Many unfortunate captains who have met with disaster will pay handsomely to be sent home again, or their masters will. Why, even now one such is here in this house, being treated by the doctor there—a glass of wine with you, Doctor! And I could tell you of others, even another navy officer—"

There was a quiet cough and Mr. Meade pushed his chair back. "I must beg to be excused," he whispered. "An indisposition."

Gille instantly turned to du Pont. "My friend, you have taken a little more wine than you should," he said coldly.

Color drained from du Pont's face, and his bulging eyes threatened to pop out of his face. He mumbled something I could not understand and fell silent, pale and staring at the table.

Meade rose and left us. Gille sighed. "I think you understand the nature of my offer," he said. "I would not have put it so crudely, perhaps."

Hunter raised his glass and took a sip of wine—a very small sip, I noticed. "Sometimes we sailors have slow wits," he said. "I cannot blame Monsieur du Pont for wanting to make it all clear." M. du Pont shot him a pathetically grateful glance as the captain continued, "It is a tempting offer, Monsieur Gille, aye, and a handsome one. But you know how it is with we who sail on account. Our crews must agree to every important decision. Therefore, if I may have, say, a week to discuss this matter with them—"

Gille spread his hands. "Take as much time as you need," he said. "And at the end of it, I hope your decision is one that will take you safely out of the harbor and back to sea."

I saw my uncle's jaw tighten, for he was quick to spot a threat, no matter how delicately uttered. When we left the table, he went to consult with his patient, though he did not take me along. When my uncle returned, M. Gille summoned a carriage to take us back to town. By that time it was quite dark, still oppressively hot, and silent except for the rioting sounds of tropical insects.

Not a word did any of us speak until the carriage set us down, at Mr. Hunter's direction, on the waterfront. Hunter had set up living quarters in a palmetto-thatched hut near one of the warehouses.

Into this we went, a mean little one-room dwelling. Hunter had slung a hammock in one corner and had set his table in the center, and around this we sat as he lit a lantern and hung it from a hook in the low ceiling.

"By heaven," Hunter growled as he sat down, "this is unendurable! Captain Brixton, not in his right mind and a prisoner! And that fool du Pont babbling, bragging of another Royal Navy officer in custody somewhere in this den of thieves! They must be rescued, I tell you."

In a quiet, urgent voice, my uncle said, "Aye, and may they be! But I tell you plain, Brixton's life is balanced on the edge of a razor. I let daylight into his brain, man! He has fever, and he is pitiably weak down his right side—'tis a mercy he's not entirely paralyzed. To move him now would be to kill him, as surely as putting a bullet into his head. And this other officer, now, where is he? Who is he? We must know before we act."

Hunter gave him an angry look. "But to do nothing—"

"And who says we do nothing?" My uncle leaned back, looking weary in the ruddy glow of the hanging lantern. Moths, which seemed always present in the islands, had found it and were whirling about the light. For a moment, Uncle Patch leaned his head back and stared at them. Then he spoke again: "Listen to me, William. We have spent five whole months in building a reputation as pirates. It would be the pity of the world to shatter that illusion now, out of sheer impatience. We may yet save Brixton and the other prisoner, but for the love of heaven, let us do it wisely and cautiously, with none of this mad rush to the guns. There are ways and there are ways, my friend."

Hunter took a deep breath, but he glared at both of us. "Very well. I am listening."

My uncle leaned forward, his voice soft and earnest. "Then listen well. Now, it seems to me that the first step, the very first one, is to learn who this other officer is and where he is held—"

And with Hunter nodding agreement and me fighting exhaustion and the call of sleep, Uncle Patch talked on, far into the night.

CHAPTER FIVE

My Discovery

Do not lose hope. Rescue is near. Be prepared.
                              —A Friend

I SIGHED AND SHOOK A SPLASH of fine
sand from the sand shaker over the words I had
just written. Then I shook the sand off and added
the page to the pile by my side. By my count I had
done two round dozen of the blessed things.

For three days, my uncle, Captain Hunter, and all
the crew who weren't patching the Aurora had been
scouring Cayona Town, hoping for news of M. du
Pont's mysterious other British officer. My part,
much to my annoyance, was to copy the letter they

were to slip to the captive if and when they found him. Captain Hunter informed me it was a very important duty since, while his men were all brave and true, most of them thought their names were spelled with an *X*. In his usual charming way, Uncle Patch warned me that I was to plant my breeches in the room and under no circumstances was I to move.

So I scraped and copied and sprinkled and stacked. It was deadly dull because the captain insisted they all be neat and legible and exactly the same. When my fingers cramped, I would brush and clean my clothing and shoes, just to have something to do. In the heat of the day I dozed, taking what the Spanish called a *siesta*.

The rest of the time I was bored. I even started to read some of Uncle Patch's precious medical books he had brought ashore with him. *Wiseman on Surgery* was one, I recall, and in it was an account of the very operation my uncle had done upon poor Captain Brixton. It was almost interesting until I realized that reading the books was precisely what my uncle hoped I would do. As much as I hate to admit it, I spent a great deal of my time sulking and feeling quite sorry for myself.

From talking to the crew every night after they returned from the ship, I knew that the search was not going well. The town, the port, the ships in the harbor—none of them yielded any news. Mr. Adams said that everything was just sealing up, like a great oyster protecting a pearl. "Something's going on, though," he concluded. "The people of Tortuga are afraid of something."

"Of what?" I asked him.

"Aye, that's the nub of it. What? I have the feeling that the people of town are so on edge, they barely are talking to one another, let alone to strangers."

The night that Mr. Adams said these words, I came to a conclusion of my own. The problem was they were sending men to do a boy's job. So the people of Cayona were suspicious of English sailors, were they? I had an answer to that.

I went through my uncle's chest until I found a fine piece of parchment he had saved just because he truly hated to throw anything away. In his portable writing-desk I found a stick of red sealing wax. I carefully wrote out my message one more time, then neatly folded the parchment into three sections and closed it with a large dollop of the hot red wax. Before it could cool, I pressed into it the Spanish coin that Sir Henry Morgan had given me as a good-luck piece. When I took the coin away, the parchment looked like a sealed, official document.

I calculated that the French of this island might not want to talk to a pirate, especially an English pirate. But a not-too-bright ship's boy, afraid he'd be beaten if he failed to deliver his scrap of fine parchment with its fine seal, well, him they might talk to.

My plan was simple. I would dress myself in my most ragged clothes, clutch my letter in my grubby hand, pull my hat down over my eyes, and just tell everyone I saw that I had a message for a British officer and did anyone know where one was?

So the next day, I waited for my uncle Patch to go stamping out, had two hard-boiled eggs and a chunk of almost fresh bread for breakfast, and then boldly marched out the door and into the teeming life of Tortuga.

For hours, it appeared that I would have no luck at all. Up to a likely-looking man I would go, tugging at my hat. "Beg pardon, *monsieur*, I am looking for an

English prisoner. I have an important letter for—"

A rattle of French, which most probably was, "Away with you, brat!" And sometimes I would have to duck a cuff aimed at my ear as I immediately vanished back into the crowd. I had not expected to succeed right away, but neither had I expected every third person I asked to try to thump me.

A fat, sweating merchant, beaming after successfully haggling over some bargain, was my next target. I sidled up to him and said in an imploring voice, "Please, sir, an English officer? I have a letter to deliver, but I can't remember the address. My master will beat me if—"

This one spoke English. "Out of my way!" And he had a better aim than the others. He swatted me a good one as I turned away.

"*Monsieur!*" I said, trying to sound as if he had nearly killed me. Truth to say, the kick hurt my pride more than anything else. I looked about for someone else to ask.

The marketplace of Cayona Town was a sprawling, open square, with everything in the world for sale. Booths, wagons, and stalls served for shops, and some merchants did with even less, with a tray hung round their necks or with a blanket spread on the ground. Behind them every other building seemed to be a tavern.

I stumbled over the rough cobblestones. A barrel-chested horse snorted at me. He was hauling a cart loaded with kegs that smelled of rum. My idea had seemed so simple back at the Royale, but out in the chaos of Cayona, I began to feel discouraged. Still, when I thought of Captain Brixton and reflected that some other officer might be in the same condition, I did not want to give up. I would keep looking.

Three more attempts, and no luck. Four. Five. Sure, and I was beginning to despair. At last I fetched up near a particularly villianous-looking tavern with a sheep's skull nailed to a board. I had heard some of the sailors talking of the Ram's Head, and that, I supposed, was where I was. By that time, it was afternoon, with the sun beating down and the people of the town going inside to escape the worst of the heat. Perhaps, I thought, I might have better luck if I went in as well, and so I crept into the tavern.

The room was dark and hot and smoky. Coming

from the blaze of day outside, I was nearly blind. I heartily wished I had lost my sense of smell as well. The place reeked of too many unwashed bodies and of much spilled rum and beer.

I stood blinking until the room became visible. The ceiling, like the door, was low and supported by long, heavy beams salvaged from some wreck. The smoke came from a dozen or so crude candles stuck on various surfaces. Men slumped around rough tables, playing cards or drinking. At the far end, almost lost in the gloom, was a long bar composed of boards laid across four barrels. One of the largest men I've ever seen was behind it, wiping tankards with a grubby towel. I squared my shoulders, put on my simplest look, and marched up to him. If I kept my distance, he couldn't hit me from across the bar.

"Ex . . . excuse me, sir," I began.

"Get out of my tavern," the man said, his voice revealing him to be Irish, though he had picked up an outlandish French accent that made his words strange. "Shame on you, coming in a place like this!"

"Ah, I swear by the saints that it's not for drink that I've come in," I said, putting as much of

Ireland in my own voice as I could. "Saints help me, but 'tis lost entirely I am."

"Aye, so are we all. We're but lambs in the wilderness, so Father Finnegan used to tell us."

Was he making fun of me? I could not tell. Still, he had made no motion to hit me. "'Tis a letter I'm to deliver, to an Englishman, a naval officer he is. Needing help from his friends, so he is, and him a prisoner among these French and all. My master gave me a silver penny to put this letter from his friends into his own hands, but his name I've forgot, and the place I've forgot. The parchment doesn't have the blessed address written on it, nor the name. I dare not open it, for 'tis sealed. So if it pleases your lordship, p'rhaps ye could help a poor Irish lad, so his English captain may not beat him cruelly?"

Small, sleepy eyes regarded me out of that vast face. On the *Louisa* on the trip over from England, a great whale had surfaced near us and I had seen those same eyes. They had a deep-buried intelligence that told you to mind your manners or something would get stove in. I gulped and babbled to a stop.

"Where was the place of your birth, lad?" the tavern keeper asked me.

"Brighton, in England," I said, knowing somehow that it was not worth lying. "But my father and my mother were both from County Clare, him a Shea and my mother a Sullivan, and they grew up within a good day's walk of the Ciffs of Moher."

"County Clare, is it?" he said. "Hm. I'm a Doolan, myself, and I do remember some Sheas and Sullivans." He leaned across the bar. "A Royal Navy officer, say ye? And your master's an Englishman, is he? Beat ye if ye fail in your errand?"

"I fear so," I said.

He sighed again. "Well, I'm probably a *gran' fou*. But if you're a Shea from County Clare—well, ye heard it not here lad, but if I was lookin' for an English prisoner hereabout, I'd go to the Commodore's."

"That was the place," I said, letting relief flood into my face. "Now, where would I find it?"

Something like a smile flashed across that wide face. "Oh, a clever lad like yourself will have little trouble finding it. Anyone can tell ye that."

I thanked him and bolted from that vile place,

but I felt his deep, heavy eyes on me the whole way out—and halfway down the street, truth be told.

The tavern keeper was right: It was easier to get directions than answers. In short order, I was standing outside of the Commodore's. It was a grim, forbidding fortress of a house, dating from the brief English occupation of Tortuga. There were no windows on the ground floor, and the ones on top were more like gun slits than true windows. A wall made of the cement-and-shell mixture called tabby surrounded it, pierced by an arched gateway in which two swinging iron-barred gates were set. Two men in sailor garb lounged up against the rough tabby wall with the studied slouch of guards everywhere.

I was trying to figure out what I should do next when a loud banging came from inside the house. One of the guards shrugged, produced an iron key on a chain, and laboriously unlocked first the gate, then the door. It was pushed open, and a scarecrow stumbled out.

At least it looked like a scarecrow. The boy who stood between the two guards was short and almost painfully slim. He was dressed in midshipman's togs about two sizes too large for him. His outfit was topped by a straw hat, like the ones the cane-cutters wove to keep the sun from their heads in the field. That covered most of his face. On his shoulders was a yoke from which dangled two wooden buckets.

The guard who'd opened the door snorted with derision. His English was so bad, I could hardly understand what he said, but I caught the words "another bath," and the whole sentence sounded like a question.

"Aye," the boy answered in a high, rough voice. "The lieutenant said—"

The other one shook his head and grumbled in French. Then he said, "Too much bathing, it makes the head soft!"

The other guard laughed. "Then yours must be like a rock!"

His friend made a rude gesture, then swept a hand at the boy. "*Allez, allez!*"

The boy lowered his head and scuttled through the gateway. I moved to follow. Lieutenant! Not a pirate rank at all. I had found the mysterious prisoner. Now to make contact.

I followed the boy up the street to a public fountain, where he set to work filling his buckets. No one seemed to pay him the least attention, so I came up beside him and whispered, "Are you English?"

He froze as if turned to stone. Slowly, he nodded his head, staring resolutely into the fountain.

"I come from an English ship," I told him. "Tell me true—is there an English prisoner in that place you came from?"

Still not turning around, he nodded again. For a second, I did not think he was going to speak, but then in a strange, rusty voice, he said, "My master is Lieutenant Fairfax. They keep him on the second floor."

I slipped my note into his hand. "Here. Hide this and give it to your master as soon as you get back. We will need to make plans—do they let you out other than to fetch water?"

The boy gave a stiff nod. "Market," he grunted. "Every midmorning."

"Then I shall met you at the market tomorrow. Have you a name? Mine's Davy Shea."

He made a sound like a gulp. Then he blurted, "Michael. My name is Michael."

"I'll see you in the market square tomorrow, then, Michael. Tell the lieutenant that friends are near."

I turned and hurried away toward the harbor. Behind me I could hear Michael filling his other bucket at the fountain. He was a strange one, for a fact. But being penned up in a prison with a fastidious lieutenant and surrounded by pirates might have had something to do with that. I doubted that I was still the same as I had been back in June, when I showed up at my uncle's with only the clothes on my back.

"Davy! Lord bless, me, but you're in a power o' trouble!" I spun around at the words, and there behind me stood Abel Tate. He was trying to scowl at me, but he could not keep a grin from twitching through. "Your uncle is that put out with ye, lad. He's got half the crew searchin' for his missin' nevvy."

"Missing!" I said. "Sure, and I'm not missing at all, for here I stand."

Tate clapped a hand on my shoulder. "Try that on your uncle, an' see what he says. Stand by for heavy weather, Davy. I've been dead and come back to life, and I'd not face him, he's that wrathful."

As Abel Tate led me back to harbor, he told me of his and the other sailors' adventures in the town. They hadn't found the missing officer—in truth, I was not surprised at that—but they had learned a few things.

Every ship in the harbor was victualing and loading powder and shot as fast as she could. It was as if an organized fleet was preparing to sail. Word was running through town that the *Concepción*, the great Spaniard we'd fought weeks ago, was patrolling the west end of the Windward Passage and had taken her fourth prize, an unlucky French privateer brig called the *Chanticleer*. She was effectively blocking the channel between the western tip of Hispaniola and the eastern shore of Cuba.

And there were rumors of another warship lurking somewhere to the north of the island, a great shadowy shape seen running across the horizon. All those who had seen her could say for certain was that she was big.

Anyone who had gone closer, Tate told me, had not returned to say anything at all.

CHAPTER SIX

A Surprise Ashore

THE NEXT DAY WE refloated the *Aurora*. Into the harbor she slipped, and there she rocked, strangely high in the water with all her cargo and guns still ashore. The first things back aboard were Captain Hunter's table and chairs in the stern cabin, and there it was that my uncle, the captain, and I met to discuss my news.

"We know two things," Hunter said. "The first is that something is up in Tortuga. It's plain that there are more pirates here and, more openly, than there should be. And the second is that we have two Englishmen to save." He nodded at me. "And that's entirely thanks to Davy, here."

My uncle gave me a fiery stare of displeasure. "Thanks to Davy, indeed! 'Tis a good thing you took the trouble not to tell me what ye were about," he declared. "For, sure, I would have warmed your breech for you!"

"He's a brave lad, Patch," Hunter put in with a smile. "While I was still planning and plotting, he took matters into his own hands, and did handsomely, I believe."

My uncle's face flamed red. He turned on Hunter and loosed words at him like a broadside: "Aye, ye may grin and grin, and think 'tis fine sport to send Davy into danger, but mark me, Hunter, one of these days you'll sail too close to the wind for your own good. 'Tis well enough to be careless of your own life—don't throw Davy's away as well."

"Now, now," Hunter said calmly. His voice took on a note of authority that I had not heard there before. "Davy's a part of the crew as much as I am—or you, for that matter. And crewmates stick together and act for the good of the ship, or else they all go to the bottom. Davy's done no harm, and he's done us a power of good. Now we have a name and a place for our mysterious captive."

"And what is the next step, sir?" I asked.

Hunter was sitting at his table, back again in the *Aurora*'s cabin. Behind him, through the stern windows, I could see Tortuga Harbor, where dozens of sloops, brigs, and barks bobbed at anchor. If half of them were pirate vessels, I thought then, there must be thousands of pirates assembled here. Captain Hunter reached for pen, ink, and paper. "Now, Davy, you will take another note—"

"That he shall not!" bellowed my uncle. "If it comes to that, I shall bear the note myself. Or send Adams, or one of the men—"

Hunter shook his head. "But they wouldn't get away with it, for we are watched, aye, and closely watched at that. Have you not noticed that the servant Cesar is always within sight when you are on land?"

My uncle looked stunned. "He has been following me?"

"Aye," said the captain. "And I have my shadow, and Mr. Adams has his, and so on. When one of us sets a foot in Cayona, Monsieur Gille soon hears of it."

"But if we are all watched—"

Captain Hunter shook his head. "Not all. Alone of us all, so far as I know, the boy is not."

Uncle Patch simply glared at him, his chest rising and falling. "And how do you know that?"

Hunter began to scribble away. "I know it because as the French watch us, we are watching them, of course. Give me credit for some sense, Patch. Besides, what is one boy in a busy place like Cayona? I'd wager sovereigns to sand dollars that not one Frenchman ashore would even remember Davy's face half a minute after passing him by. To Gille, he is a servant, nothing more. You have never mentioned that Davy is your nephew, not in his hearing."

"He could learn that from any member of the crew," insisted my uncle with a sullen, dogged air.

"Aye, if he were interested in servants. But he is not, and my men would not tell. Nor will Morgan's, I think, for Sir Henry chose the smartest heads among his old crews to fill our crew."

It took some wrangling, but when I pointed out that I was going only to the market square, not to the house itself, at last my uncle began to give in a bit. And finally I found just the way to cap off my argument: "Uncle," said I, "you thought me man enough when I held Captain Brixton's head still as you peeled back his scalp and sawed into his living skull. Am I not man enough then to run an errand?"

Hunter had just finished his note. As he sprinkled sand on the page to dry the ink, he glanced shrewdly up at my uncle, who stood with arms crossed, leaning against a locker. "That was well said, Patch. And how do you answer?"

Through clenched teeth, my uncle said, "To the devil with it! Have your way, then, for between the two of ye, you have not sense enough to have a care for your own skins. But no tricks, mind, Davy! It's straight to the market you go, and put the blasted note into the hands of this Michael, and then whip back to the ship again!"

"Yes, sir," I said, but taking care not to make it a promise of any kind.

Captain Hunter folded the message and reached for a stick of sealing wax. He melted this in the candle flame and sealed his paper. He held it up, waving it in the air. "Now, the first note I sent said nothing but that we were friends to this captive. This one makes a more open offer of aid. But look you, Davy, don't say a word of our being anything, not pirate ship, not a letter of marque, nothing. We know nothing of this Lieutenant Fairfax, and the less he knows of us, the better it will be for all." He handed over the letter.

"Aye, sir," I said and, tucking the paper inside my shirt, I left them there.

What the two had said about our crew's being watched had put me on edge. That trip was a jumpy one, for, sure, I imagined prying eyes everywhere and saw danger on all sides—in the annoyed glance of a mule driver passing by; the raised eyebrows of a woman gazing out of a window; the way people behind me spoke, it seemed to me, in whispers. I imagined that Monsieur Gille or even the governor of Tortuga had set spies everywhere, and that I was the center of their interest.

But that notion jostled clean out of my head in the market, where all was noise and bustle and haggling. Through the crowds I moved, darting like a minnow through seaweed, and staring about all the time for Michael. What I saw mostly was French waistcoats and shirts, and barrows of mangoes, of bread, of dried fish, of bright knives gleaming in the sun, of deadly little pistols. There were people selling living meat: pigeons in cages (for they came in great numbers to Tortuga in the wintertime, and they ate well, plump and tender), pigs miserable in the heat, even goats bleating their displeasure. Before long, it was plain even to me that no spy could keep track of one boy in all that throng, and then I breathed a little easier.

At last I caught sight of a familiar skinny figure and, dodging through the crowd, I came alongside him. "I have something for you," I said in a whisper that probably was drowned out even from his ears in the rattle and roar of the marketplace.

Without a word, he ducked through the crowd and into a narrow side street, hardly more than an alley. For the moment, I did not know what to make of this at all. Was he afraid we'd be caught? Was perhaps *he* being watched? Despite the heat, I almost shivered, and I felt the hair rising on the back of my neck. But then I saw Michael twitch his shoulder in a way that said "follow me" as plain as words, and I sidled around, looking at a cart of swords. Glancing to the left and right, I tried to seem as though I were thinking of buying a blade, but really I was checking to see whether anyone was noticing me. No one was, so I trailed down the alley after him. He stood at the far end, and he jerked his head toward yet another narrow, dark passage. He came to light in a deep, arched door-way, and I slipped in beside him. "Someone watching?" I asked.

"Never know," he growled in his strange, hoarse voice.

I reached into my shirt. "This is for the lieu-tenant. My captain says he's willing to help."

The folded paper passed from me to him, and then vanished somewhere inside his rags. He was wearing his outlandish great straw hat with a wide brim, and this hid most of his face from me. Indeed, since he seemed interested only in his toes and looked down at them the whole time, all I could see of him was the tip of his chin. He carried a straw basket, too, and this he raised as he said, "I'm to buy fruit."

Thinking that if one boy would pass unnoticed, two could scarcely be more obvious, I tagged along back to the market. Michael had a few words of French—mainly "*Non!*" whenever a cart owner named a price—and they served well enough for him to collect so many papayas, melons, and mangoes that the basket drooped with the weight of them. He had a few silver pieces, and these diminished as the basket grew heavier. At last he said, "This is enough." We left the market square behind, and he growled, "Where are you going?"

"I'll help you carry it," said I, "for it's a heavy burden."

Taking turns about lugging the basket, we walked through twisting, rutted streets until we came to the cleared ground around the Commodore's. The two guards standing beside the door were not the same men I had seen earlier, but they looked no less bored and no less cruel.

One of them said something sour and angry in a rush of French. Michael shook his head. The other gave him a rough swat. In heavily accented English, the second guard snarled, "He says what does the English do with so much fruit, eh?"

"Eats it," said Michael, staring sullenly at the ground.

The other man took the basket from me and went through it, making sure we were smuggling in no twenty-four-pound cannon, I suppose. He said something else.

The other guard translated: "Who is this boy?"

"The basket's heavy. I asked him to help. My master will give him a penny."

The first guard plucked a mango from the basket, smashed it against the wall, and bit into the flesh, juice trickling down over his chin. He thrust the basket back at me, and I took it. "Be quick," the English-speaking guard snarled, helping Michael and me through the gate with a kick apiece.

Inside the gate, Michael rasped, "Did you *have* to come?"

"Sure, and I'd like the penny," I replied, maybe a bit too smartly.

Approaching the Commodore's, I thought how fortlike it looked, with its heavy walls and musket-slit windows. The front door was a tight squeeze, as if made for easy defense from within. Just inside the doorway was a narrow winding stair, and up this we went, emerging into the one big room that made up the entire top floor of the house.

It was as dark as could well be in the noontime,

for the narrow windows let but little light in, but it was cooler than I had expected. The shadowy room looked shabby enough. In a corner was a homely China chamber pot, and together with a drunkenly leaning table, a narrow straight chair, and a broken-down sofa, this was the whole of the furniture. Two tattered and worn hammocks were slung in the corners opposite the door, but these were empty.

Lying stretched out on the sofa, dressed in black slippers, loose white trousers, and a loose gray shirt, lay a figure fanning himself with a palm frond. To my eye he looked oddly lazy. He raised himself on one elbow, staring at us. I had no doubt he could see the two of us better than we could him, because our eyes were still dazzled by the bright sunlight outside. "Who is this?" asked the stranger in a surprisingly soft English voice.

To my surprise, Michael dashed his straw hat to the floor, snatched up the chamber pot—fortunately empty—and hurled it straight at my head. I dodged, and it smashed against the wall behind me. "Who is it?" raged Michael in a voice I knew, all hoarseness and whispering gone. "Who is it? It's a pirate, that's who it is! It's a renegade, a jailbreaker, a . . . a . . . a great *mooncalf!*"

Mooncalf?

Only one person had ever called me that.

Staring at the boy, I felt as if the scales had fallen from my eyes, like the blind man in the Bible. And then I knew, and I could not help crying aloud the true name of "Michael."

"Saints in heaven! Jessie Cochran!" I said.

Lieutenant Fairfax stood up and ordered us to speak more quietly, and then the story tumbled out. "How come you to be here?" I asked in a whisper.

Jessie sank the floor, glaring at me. Now that I knew her, I wondered how she had ever fooled me, for there were her freckles, and her brown hair, and all that I remembered so well. "I come to be here," she said bitterly, "because my mother thought Port Royal wasn't safe enough for me!"

"Quietly," warned the lieutenant.

Jessie pointed to the china fragments in the corner. "If they didn't hear that, they won't hear us talking."

It was a good point, I thought. Jessie looked almost as if she was about to cry when she mentioned her mother. Moll Cochran was a widow and the owner of The King's Mercy Inn in Port Royal. 'Twas there I had lived with my uncle during the previous summer, up until we joined Captain Hunter and sailed away pretending to be pirates. "I don't understand," I said.

Jessie shrugged. "People talked about us after you and your uncle left, for they knew he had lodged there. And it's a rough town, crammed with sailors who drink too much and don't mind their manners. So last fall we found it hot for us, what with the navy sailors angry with us for giving house room to a pirate. Trade fell off, and times were hard."

"We meant no harm to you," I said.

"And I'm glad you and your uncle got away," she replied half-grudgingly. In truth, Jessie had actually helped me as much as she could when I had gone to free my uncle from jail. "Then my mother learned that Lady Wellesley, whose husband, Sir Milo, had just died, was sailing back to England, for her own health was not good. Lady Wellesley was a highborn woman, but she was kind to my mother, and my mother asked her to take me in service as her maid, to get me passage back to England. There I was to live with my aunt and learn how to be"—she almost spat the words— "more genteel."

Fairfax had sat back down on the sofa, leaning forward with his arms crossed on his chest. He took up the tale: "They shipped aboard the *Venture*, my packet. But Lady Wellesley suddenly died a week into the voyage. Then, south of Bermuda, we were taken by a pirate ship. On my instructions, Jessie disguised herself as a boy, and when they took all the officers prisoner, she came with me as my servant."

"Why?" I asked. "Why not stay with the packet?"

Jessie snorted. "With all the officers gone, and the sailors left alone and in charge? I'd sooner take my chances here!"

Fairfax glanced toward the door. "We haven't much time. The guards will come in if you don't leave soon. What's afoot?"

Remembering my errand, I said, "Mich—Jessie has a letter for you, sir. My captain will do all in his power to help you escape. You and Jessie together."

Shaking his head, Fairfax said, "I'm not sure that can be done. The pirate who took our ship is not alone in this. He has a master, a man named Gille—what's the matter?"

"I know the man," I said. "And I know he is holding another English prisoner as well, a Captain Brixton."

The name seemed to mean nothing to Fairfax, which struck me as a little odd, for the British Navy was not numerous here, and all of them knew the others. "Whatever the case, Gille has money and power. And men. If he wanted to man this place like a fort, it would take an army to break into it. The only reason the guard is so light is that I cannot climb through these windows, and if I got downstairs, I could not climb over the wall around the yard. A word from Gille, and this house would become a stronghold."

"Listen," I said, "Gille wants my captain to sail for him. That won't happen—for reasons I can't tell you. But the two of them are talking to each other. That may give us a chance. I'll tell the captain your situation. Keep tight and quiet here until we get word back to you." I turned to Jessie. "Can you find some excuse to go to the market every day?"

"Or to the fountain for water," she said. She sniffed. "You didn't even know me. You really are a mooncalf."

"Then arrange it to go to the fountain at noon every day. When we have a plan, I'll meet you there. Be ready to act!"

When I went back down, I clutched a bright penny. One of the guards relieved me of it and gave me a kick into the bargain, but I hardly minded. It just gave me that much more speed back to the ship and back to the captain.

CHAPTER SEVEN

The Rescue

CAPTAIN HUNTER AT once set about devising a plan. He said we had to free both Captain Brixton and Lieutenant Fairfax at the same time, and nothing less would do. In a way, it made sense, for once we had made an attempt to bring away one of them, Tortuga would be too hot for us to remain and try for the other.

Still, Uncle Patch had his own ideas on that subject. "You do realize that this is a foolish enterprise, don't ye, William?"

"Foolish it may be," said Hunter doggedly, pacing the wharf near the *Aurora*. The men had almost finished restowing all her cargo, and we had only to fill her casks with water to be ready to sail. That made the necessity for action all the keener, as Hunter saw things. "Still, Doctor, even a fool can hear the call of duty."

"Well, well," grumbled my uncle. "I can only ask you not to get us all killed, I suppose. Though Lord knows that's the last worry a hothead like yourself would have!" Uncle Patch did persuade the captain that charging in with pistols firing and cutlasses flashing was probably not the best way to achieve success.

I stayed quiet and listened to them debate. Finally, the plan they came up with was better thought out but would call for careful timing, courage . . . "And the luck of the devil himself," my uncle finished, "for 'tis a certainty that never a saint would concern himself with such a scheme as this."

And so that Friday, the tenth of February, I found myself seated next to the captain in M. Gille's fine carriage once again on our way to dine. Hunter was in full pirate dress: his rich emerald green coat with the red piping and frogs; the amazing canary yellow sash; and black boots that shone like mirrors. He had a new wig he had picked up in the marketplace.

It was the sort called a court-wig, like the ones the king's counselors wore: black and curled and falling to his shoulders. As my uncle had remarked, you could buy anything there. Still, I did wonder about the fate of the wig's former owner—did he still even have a head to call his own? His hat with the ostrich plume the captain held in his lap, for with the wig and the low carriage roof, he couldn't put it on his head.

"Are you sure this is going to work, sir?" I asked, running my finger inside my tight collar.

"We must trust to fortune, Davy. All we have to do is follow the plan and all will be well. At least that's what your uncle Patch said."

Aye, my uncle Patch. Having raged and roared at the idiocy of even attempting what Captain Hunter wanted to do, my dear uncle had thrown himself into logistics and strategies. Even now, no doubt with him grumbling all the way, he and two crewmen fluent in French were headed for the Commodore's. The sailors bore two jugs of the finest brandy from the *Aurora*'s stores. Both had been spiked with tincture of opium, a sleeping agent that Uncle Patch swore by. Of course, Uncle Patch swore by and at everything.

My uncle was willing to wager that two cheerful French-speaking sailors, free with their drink, would be able to persuade the guards to take a dram. And that was all that would be needed, for if they worked it right, both guards would be blissfully asleep within minutes. The plan was for the sailors to take their places while Uncle Patch spirited Lieutenant Fairfax and Jessie out of that grim place and made them safe aboard the *Aurora*.

That would only leave the rescue of Captain Brixton. This would be up to that notorious pirate, Mad William Hunter, and myself. The captain was actually looking forward to it, for there was nothing he enjoyed more than this kind of deceit. Had he not gone to sea, I thought, he would have made a fine play-actor upon the stage. For myself, I thought such acting was close to lying.

And I feared I was getting too good at it.

Night was falling fast when we arrived at the plantation house. The white, square stone building was ablaze with candlelight. "Beeswax candles," Hunter murmured, pointing out the golden gleam. "None of your cheap tallow dips for our grand Monsieur Gille!" Captain Hunter smiled with satisfaction. I couldn't help thinking that the windows all looked like hot yellow eyes, silent predators waiting patiently for us to enter their den. But I squared my shoulders and followed him in like a good servant.

If anything, this meal was even more opulent than the last. The table was covered in heavy white silk and laid out with fine patterned china and silver worth a rich Spanish prize. The food was all French: fish and vegetables in colorful, fragrant glazes and sauces. The smell was tantalizing, and my mouth would have watered had it not been so dry with fear of the Frenchmen at the table.

M. Gille sat in his grand chair, dressed in rich purples and blood reds. His round, smooth face glistened in the candlelight, none of which seemed to reach his dark eyes. To his right sat not M. du Pont but Mr. Meade, his English manager. Slim, quiet, and still dressed in his subdued browns, he would have disappeared completely into shadows were it not for his long white wig. It was almost possible to forget he was there, so silent he remained.

Captain Hunter made small talk through the first part of the meal. At the first remove, a servant poured some pale wine for him, filling a fine Venetian crystal goblet. Captain Hunter lifted it and stared at the candlelight through the wine as he swirled the glass. "I have given your kind offer of, ah, partnership, considerable thought, Monsieur Gille, as have my men."

M. Gille dabbed at his lips with a napkin and gave Hunter a simpering smile. "Indeed, Captain Hunter. And have all of you come to a conclusion?"

Hunter sipped the wine and nodded appreciatively. "Very fine, sir. Come to a conclusion? Indeed, I believe we have, sir."

You might have sliced the tension in the air with a carving knife. As I studied M. Gille's face, I became aware that something had changed since our last meeting. What had the planter discovered about us? What had his spies reported? Sweat was trickling down my back, and I wanted to scratch more than anything.

M. Gille lifted his own wineglass and took a sip in obvious imitation of Captain Hunter. "Ah, yes, most delightful. And may one ask what your conclusion is, then?"

Hunter shrugged. "The only sensible one, as you

have so kindly pointed out to me, Monsieur Gille. Shall we sign articles?"

There was a polite cough, and Mr. Meade dabbed his pale lips with his napkin. "Forgive Monsieur Gille if he does not speak personally. I hope your speaking of signing articles is meant metaphorically, sir. A written arrangement is out of the question. Your agreement must necessarily be informal. I am sure you understand."

With a chuckle, Hunter said, "Then it's the word of honor of gentlemen of fortune, is it? It will do for me if it will do for you."

"That is rather the question," Mr. Meade said delicately, the candlelight catching his eyes for just a second. I wished they hadn't.

"I do not understand your meaning, sir," Captain Hunter said, letting a hint of danger slip into his voice. Here we go, I thought, with the heart of me climbing into my throat. Uncle Patch had planned for this moment. I hoped he had planned well.

"The meaning, Captain Hunter," rumbled M. Gille, "is that I have, how do you say, developed concerns about the wisdom of a joint venture.

People in port know little about you or your ship. Oh, we know you have taken prizes, and we have the enthusiastic affidavits of Captain Barrel on your bravery. It is your *raisons*, your motives, that give me pause."

Hunter turned his head slowly. "My motives, sir?"

Gille toyed with his goblet. "Your crew has been asking questions in Cayona, sir. Questions of a naval nature."

Captain Hunter grinned, looking like a blond wolf. A slight frown formed on Gille's smooth brow. He did not speak, though, and Hunter smoothly began to talk: "So it's like that, is it? Fine, then, let's clear the decks! Did you think that I wouldn't know? Did you really think that Patch wouldn't tell me?"

Gille glanced at Meade, who said nothing. The Frenchman said, "I do not know what you—"

"Brixton!" Hunter snapped, rising like wrath from his chair. "Your precious English guest is Alexander Brixton, late of His Majesty's frigate *Retribution*! I thought when she was blown to perdition, she took that smug pig with her!"

"You know him?" M. Gille asked, sounding more confused than angry.

"Know him! He ruined my career with his brutality and harshness! Branded me mutineer, tried to hang me like a side of beef, tried to blow me and mine out of Port Royal Harbor when we made good our escape!" The captain was breathing hard now, eyes wide and blazing. "So you think I have some connection with the navy still, do you? Right. Then let us put that to rest! Brixton is alive, and the only reason he would be is for ransom."

"Captain Hunter," warned Mr. Meade, "you cannot expect my employer to answer that. His position—"

"To blazes with his position!" roared Hunter. "But let me tell you this: The old buzzard has no family and no fortune. You'll get nothing for him. But by now you should know that. However, you may be willing to sell him." Hunter yanked a purse loose from his belt and threw it on the table. It landed with a heavy clink, spilling its contents, and the candlelight caught the sunlight gleam of minted gold. I held my breath.

In the sudden silence, I could hear a faint whistle

of breath in Gille's nostrils. He did not even glance at the gold, but kept his gaze fixed on the captain.

Hunter sank easily back into his chair and tossed back half his wine. "There's my offer. Sell him to me, and I'll take him off your hands."

"You wish revengement," Gille said. "I think I see. But the good Doctor Shea says his patient might not survive, even with his ministrations."

With as ghastly a leer as I ever hope to see, Hunter leaned forward. "That devil Brixton ruined Dr. Shea along with the rest of us. Patch is an excellent surgeon. He can keep a man alive for days. Even when he doesn't want to be!" Hunter leaned further into the candlelight. "Is it a bargain?"

M. Gille stared at him coldly. Then his eyes took the slightest twitch to the right, where Mr. Meade sat in his shadows. Did I imagine it or did that white wig nod slightly in return? No matter, M. Gille smiled. "I believe we can do business, Captain Hunter. Would you prefer to discuss terms now?"

"Aye, but first things first. Davy!" Captain Hunter turned to me. The wolfish smile was still on his face, and his eyes were wild. "Run you to the ship and tell Mr. Adams to attend me here. Have him bring some men. Tell him we'll be taking away some merchandise!"

"Aye, aye, sir!" I squeaked and took to my heels. The house seemed much larger going out than coming in as I pelted for the door. I was through it in a flash and running down the drive and through the gates. It was only when they were safely out of sight behind me that I paused to get my breath. Uncle Patch's mad plan had actually worked! I could hear his conspiratorial whisper in my mind: "Give 'em a kernel of truth wrapped in a parcel of lies, and buy the old man!"

But then I heard something that had been no part of my uncle's plan: the tramp of many feet coming up the road. I hid myself in the woods just in time to avoid a patrol of sailors coming up from town. They were rough-looking men with drawn cutlasses, marching along behind a bulky bald man whose head seemed to be covered in tattoos. As soon as they were past, I took to the road and raced toward the Commodore's, where the rescue of Jessie and Lieutenant Fairfax should have been well underway.

I breathed a sigh of relief when I arrived at the

Commodore's and saw that the guards at the gate were two sailors from the *Aurora*. One of them leveled his musket as I came running up.

"Put that down! 'Tis I, Davy Shea! I've got to see my uncle Patch!"

"'Tain't loaded," muttered Abel Tate. "The doctor is—"

"Right behind you," Uncle Patch snarled as he stood framed in the archway. Quickly, I informed him of all that had happened. He didn't seem pleased. "What's Hunter playing at? I warned him to string it out, to keep them debating until midnight or later."

"But we didn't expect Monsieur Gille to doubt us!" I said, trying to defend the captain.

"And us with such honest faces and all. I'll see to the men he needs. You go upstairs and see if the lieutenant and his ragged servant are ready. The guards are asleep in the yard, and we caught them as they came on duty, so we've nearly four hours to spare."

The two guards lay just inside the gate, breathing heavily. I rushed past them and up the stair. Lieutenant Fairfax had changed into clothes that

Uncle Patch must have brought with him: canvas trousers, linen shirt, a vest, and a scarf tied around his head. The disguise was topped off with a black eye patch that he was shifting from eye to eye as if looking for the best effect. It all made him look very young, like a child playing at dress-up.

I was still staring at him when Jessie Cochran came up and hit me hard on the arm. "What are you doing here?" she demanded.

"Faith, that hurts, Jessie!" I complained, rubbing my arm. "Listen, now. I've come fresh from Gille's plantation, and my uncle says to—"

That was as far as I got before the lieutenant was next to me, demanding to know every detail of what had happened. So I was forced to go through the whole thing, to Jessie's openmouthed amazement and the lieutenant's thoughtful nods. Then I mentioned the sailors I had passed, and the man with the tattooed head. Both grew pale at that.

"A stout man with a great barrel chest?" Fairfax asked urgently. "And the tattoos, were they all kinds of blue swirls over the top of his head?"

"I can't answer to the color, for I only saw by moonlight, but as to the swirls, aye, just as you said."

"Then we'd best hurry. That man is the captain of the *Sultana*, the pirate ship that took the *Venture* and landed Jessie and me in this mess."

"We don't know his true name," Jessie said breathlessly. "His crew just called him Shark. I watched him pick up one of his own wounded men and throw him over the side!"

"Come, there is not a moment to lose," Fairfax said as he buckled a borrowed sword around his waist. He no longer looked like a young boy. Now he looked like a dangerous one. "We had best make our escape so that this Captain Hunter can make his. Davy, my compliments to your terribly effective uncle Patch, and tell him we shall be right behind you. And tell him what we said about this pirate Shark."

So down the stairs I pounded, thinking that running was all I was about this day. Uncle Patch was pacing back and forth like an Irish bear, muttering curses under his breath as fast as he could draw it. I gasped out the lieutenant's compliments and the information that Captain Shark had entered the plan.

"Brimstone and blazes!" he snarled. "Sure, and

this gets better by the minute, it does! The plan sprung too soon, and now real pirates meddling into it as well!"

"Is the captain in danger?" I asked.

My uncle flapped his arms. "When have you known him not to be? I'm lumbered with that young popinjay upstairs, and until he's safely stowed, our hands are tied! I've sent Abel Tate back to fetch Mr. Adams and some of the others. Perhaps they can bluff their way in and bear Brixton back. Fly back to Gille's and let William know what's afoot. Here, you shall take my horse, the roan tied in front of the tavern yonder."

We walked to the very end of the next street, and for some minutes I stood wondering whether I dared get in the saddle at all. The beast was a snappish thick-headed brute of a hired horse, but grateful I was not to have to run the five miles back to the Gille plantation. Once I had made the climb, the fool of a horse wanted to dance about the street with me for more minutes, until I began to think it would have been faster to walk.

Finally, though, I persuaded the animal to start forward. It seemed to know the road, for it did not stumble, though several times the devil tried to throw me off. Nothing I could do would persuade it to go faster than an amble, and all in all the horse was only a trouble to me. At last I swung off the creature while still three hundred yards away from Gille's, for I had not left riding a mount, and thus wanted no questions about how I had come by one.

I meant to tie him to a tree beside the road, only the ill-natured brute yanked the reins from my hands and took off back toward the town. I stared after the beast for a moment, then turned my eyes to the sky. A few stars twinkled there, and the moon, now past full, seemed to be staring down at me. Maybe it was wondering what Davy Shea was doing, tearing about on a night full of doubt and danger such as this.

For I was myself wondering just that.

CHAPTER EIGHT

Bloodshed!

I HAD NOT REACHED the gate when I heard hoofbeats approaching. Quick as thought, I darted off the road and behind one of the trees whose gnarled roots crept in a web over the stones. I tried to melt against the trunk. The horse and rider came into view, just a dark silhouette against the gray of the moonlit road. Whoever was in the saddle was not a tall figure, and I crouched to pick up a fist-size stone to defend myself with. I might have thrown it too, had the person following me not reined in the galloping horse and called sharply, "Come out! I know you're there!"

"Jessie!" I exclaimed, dropping the stone. I

stepped out into the moonlight. "What are you doing here? What's happened?"

"Nothing's happened," she insisted, looking down at me from the back of the very horse that had run away from me minutes before. "Except that I'm coming with you."

"No, that you are not!" I exclaimed hotly. "I'll not be responsible for you!"

"Fiddle-faddle!" she shot back. "You're a fine one to talk. You're likely to get yourself killed without some help. You can't even hold on to a horse."

I felt my cheeks burning in the darkness. "I let him go," I said.

She leaped from the saddle. "Then so will I." She gave the horse a smart slap on his rump, and the beast ran away, back toward town. "Come on! We're wasting time."

"But you were supposed to go back to the ship—"

"They don't need me. Fairfax, and your uncle, and two sailors are already on their way back to the *Aurora*. You're the one I'm worried about. Can't you hurry?"

"Not without falling and breaking my head," I muttered, but we were already within sight of the tall stone wall about the house. I had been worrying about talking our way past the guard, but there was no need at all, for the gate was open and unlocked, and never a guard did we see.

We stepped into the yard. Down the tree-lined lane, the white house gleamed with light. Every room seemed to have a hundred candles in it, with the yellow glare spilling out into the hot tropical night. "Something's wrong," I said. "'Tis strange that the house is all lit up like that, and nothing afoot but supper. How did you get past my uncle?"

"I crept down and was listening in the shadows when you talked to him," she said. "While you were fooling with the horse, I got a head start on you, and you didn't even notice me half a mile back when you went riding him past. If you can call it riding! Anyway, where are the pirates?"

There she had me. Captain Shark and his men were nowhere in evidence, not that I could see. Perhaps they were in the house, or perhaps they lurked on the grounds. There was no telling, but the best path seemed to be to take our courage in our hands and boldly stroll up to the door, for I had learned that if you look as though you have some urgent business, people tend to let you be. "Come on," I said, leading the way.

We stepped onto the deserted veranda, and then I noticed that the front door stood ajar. Without knocking, I pushed it open and we stepped down the hall and into the dark entrance room. No one was there, not a soul, not a servant, not a mouse. I nodded toward the panel that concealed the sick-room and whispered, "Brixton's in there, but I don't know how to work the door at all."

"Worry about him later," returned Jessie.

We were halfway down the hall to the dining room when we heard someone swearing in French—and coming our way. "In here," Jessie whispered, grabbing me by the arm and dragging me through a doorway.

We stepped into a sort of study, with an enormous, elaborate desk and two walls that were nothing but bookshelves, floor to ceiling. French doors, closed against the night, were opposite the hall door. Beside them on either side were open windows, with filmy curtains drifting on the sultry night breeze. The whole wall behind the desk was covered by a hanging tapestry showing hunters with lances pursuing a leopard. Overhead, a chandelier blazed with candles. Jessie closed the door, and we flattened ourselves against the wall.

But then the voice stopped right outside the room, angry and loud, and I heard a rattle at the door handle. Jessie again dashed past me, tugging me along, and we dived behind the tapestry. There was barely room for us, but she lay on her stomach, and I did the same, with my head at her feet. Even so, the bottom of the tapestry pushed out from the wall, but we had at least a chance of escaping attention.

I could see only through the crack between the bottom of the tapestry and the floor, so when the door opened and three men came in, all I could glimpse were feet. The door slammed, and the French rose in pitch and in anger. It was the voice of M. Gille, and he seemed far from pleased.

A rough English voice cut him off: "Belay! I don't understand your French jabber. Talk English!"

There came a pause, and I heard Gille take three or four deep, rasping breaths. Then he spoke in English, but his tone was no less furious: "How dare you! How dare you come to this house? You know our arrangement. I cannot afford to have your ruffians visit this place so openly!"

"Business," said the rough voice shortly. "Monkey business, if ye asks me. I don't like to be cheated, not me. I don't take kindly to them what cheats me either."

"Mr. Meade," Gille said coldly, "call the servants and throw this dog out!"

"I'm afraid it's too late for that," replied Meade's soft, honeyed voice. "And Captain Shark does have a point, Monsieur."

I sensed Jessie ahead of me going stiff with surprise. Meade did not seem the type to defend a roughneck like Shark.

Gille's voice dripped with contempt: "So you are afraid of him, are you?"

"No," Meade answered slowly. "In fact, sir, I agree with him."

"He was the one who told us how much you was cheatin'," said Shark.

"And though I did not think this the best time for Captain Shark to press his arguments, I could not in all honesty tell him you would make things right," added Meade.

After a baffled silence, Gille asked, "What do you wish of me? What is your complaint?"

"Nothin' much," growled Shark. "Only that the money ye gave Meade to pay us is rather less than half o' what it should be. Blazes! If I was to take that an' call it square, why, my men would depose me in a minute, and I couldn't blame 'em if they did, not I."

"Times are hard," Gille told him. "With that devil Captain Steele threatening all trade, I'd be a fool to buy your goods at full price, not knowing whether I could ship them elsewhere for sale. But if they sell for what they should, I will add to your payment. Only when the sale is made, though!"

"Not good enough," snarled Shark. "I say ye're a lying jackal."

Gille swore in French, and I heard the hiss of a sword being drawn from its scabbard. There was a quick, sharp clash of steel on steel, a kind of gurgling gasp, and then the heavy thud of a body on the far side of the desk, where I could not see. I tried hard to press myself into the wall at my back, and to quiet the hammering of my heart.

"You've done 'im," said the rough voice of

Captain Shark. A pause, and then, "Aye, 'e's dead, all right. What next, Cap'n Steele?"

At that, my thudding heart leaped right into my mouth. Captain Steele? Here? It was as if Satan himself were striding about the study on his cloven hooves!

A soft sigh, and then Meade said, "Well, the fool's time was coming to an end anyway. I had hoped to delay this, but since it has happened, we have to deal with the others. You get some men and secure the gate. I'll go back to the dining room and tell them Monsieur Gille is detained. When you've seen to the gate, bring half a dozen men and we'll take them prisoner and see if they're worth anything. Hurry now."

"Aye."

Peering through the crack, I saw one man's feet move to the door. It opened, and the man was gone. It had to be Meade, from the elegant, silver-buckled shoes—or rather, it had to be Captain Steele!

Ahead of me, Jessie was creeping along the floor toward the wall with the French door. I reached to grab her ankle, but too late—she was standing and then she had whisked out from behind the tapestry. I had no choice but to leap to my feet and follow her.

A fearful glance showed me the fallen Gille, lying facedown in his own blood. Kneeling beside him, with his back to us, was Captain Shark, busily tugging at the dead man's coat and going through the Frenchman's pockets.

I think Jessie had believed that both men were gone. Seeing her mistake, she quickly, quietly stepped to the open window, put a leg over the sill, and slipped through. But her landing made a crunch that seemed as loud to me as the crack of doom itself!

Shark's head snapped around, quick as a serpent's strike. With an oath, he snatched up his bloodstained cutlass!

Not even thinking, I dived headfirst for the window, taking the filmy curtain with me. To my horror, the pirate was so quick that I felt his hand close on my ankle, jerking me to a stop and bringing me crashing to earth on my chin. Yellow light flashed in my eyes, and my head spun.

I did not pass out, though, and yanked my leg

hard, bracing with my other foot against the window-sill. Jessie was standing, and when she saw what was happening, she thought fast. I heard another crunch and a howl of pain, and my ankle was free. I tumbled down and sprang to my feet, tearing the curtain away from me. Jessie had slammed the window sash down on Shark's wrist, so hard that I imagined she broke some bones. His hand was caught, the fingers clenching in fury. I heard muffled curses from behind the window and knew we had to move fast.

"Come on!" I gasped, and set off at a run for the back of the house and the dining room.

Like the study, the dining room, too, had French doors. They were probably locked, but that did not stop me. Through them I could see Mr. Meade, his back to me, standing and waving his hand as he spoke to Captain Hunter. I raised my leg and gave the lock of the door an almighty flat-footed kick. The doors flew inward, glass shattering from the panes, and Jessie and I were inside, and I was yelling across the table, "Captain! Treachery! Come on!"

We hurtled past the astonished form of Mr.

Meade. Hunter threw his chair back, leaped onto the table himself, his sword already drawn and, with a whisk of the blade, he cut the rope holding the big chandelier. He had jumped to the floor and had grabbed my arm when the massive thing smashed onto the table behind him, plunging us into darkness. Glass flew everywhere. Hunter pushed me and dragged Jessie into the hall, slammed the door behind him, and jammed a chair beneath the handle. "Where's Brixton?" he demanded of me.

I pointed toward the front of the house. "There! But I don't know—"

The study door ahead of us flew open, and a wild-eyed Captain Shark lunged out, cherishing his broken right hand against his chest and brandishing his cutlass with his left. He cursed and raised the sword awkwardly, but Hunter had whipped out a pistol. It went off right beside my ear, deafening me and causing me to close my eyes in shock. When I opened them, only Shark's legs were visible, the rest of his body thrown back inside the study doorway. He must have been wounded, not killed, for he moved his legs, as if trying to get up again. Hunter pushed me again, and I jumped over the outstretched, twitching legs.

In the entry hall, I pointed to the paneling. "Behind there, but I don't know how it works!"

Hunter made no ado about that. As I had done, he kicked at the paneling, and it split beneath his boot. Another kick, and he had broken a hole the size of my head. He grabbed this, and with a grunt shoved left and right. A blow of his shoulder made something crack, and the panel gave inward.

Hunter took a step into the room and then stopped. I heard him groan.

Unlike the other rooms, this one had only one candle. In its feeble light, though, I saw ruin. Poor Captain Brixton lay stark dead upon the bed, his head thrown back and his throat cut from ear to ear. The villains must have done that when they first came into the house.

Hunter whirled and said, "There's no helping him. Out, quickly!"

By then I could hear distant shouts. We plunged out the front door into the night. A pirate, one of Shark's men, was almost to the gate. He heard us and turned, cutlass out, but Hunter was on him with a furious rain of sword-cuts. The pirate screamed for help, but in the instant that he turned his attention away, Hunter raised his sword and punched the man square in the face with the pommel, stretching him out on the ground.

"Fly!" Hunter yelled. "To the ship!"

We were through the gate and stumbling on the rutted road, but Hunter dragged Jessie and me into the woods. "This way is better," he said.

Seconds later, hoofbeats drummed past on the road. One of the pirates, I supposed, going for reinforcements.

"Sir," I panted, "Captain Steele—"

"Tell me about him later," snapped Hunter. "Across this field!"

I suppose that we ran through a tobacco field. It was planted with something that had been harvested but had left little stumps, anyway. The moon gave us just enough light to make running dangerous—what we thought was solid ground would turn out to be a hole or a stone in our path. Still, we cut across the field, through some woods, and then came out on another road. We turned left on it, toward Cayona. Some little farmhouses were scattered along our way, and as we passed them, dogs barked and once, a donkey brayed forlornly.

But we were going downhill, at least. At last we saw lights ahead, and then we were on the outskirts of town. Hunter had learned the lay of the land well. He led us at a smart clip through winding narrow alleys until we came to the very wharf where the *Aurora* lay tied. "All aboard?" he asked the astonished Mr. Gray as we hurried up the ship.

"Aye, sir, but the doctor's party is just on the point of going back for Captain Brixton," said Gray.

"He need not bother," Hunter said shortly. "Cast off, and make sail. We're minutes ahead of men who wish us ill!"

"Aye," Gray replied, and in a second he was barking orders that brought men swarming up from belowdecks.

Uncle Patch came onto the deck as well, his face showing open wonder. "What the blazes is afoot?" he demanded, his voice peevish.

"They killed Brixton," Hunter told him flatly. "I've escaped by the grace of God and the skin of my teeth. Davy's safe, and so is his friend here. How is Lieutenant Fairfax?"

"Well enough and entirely unhurt. But what the devil happened?"

"Captain Steele!" I shouted.

"Later," ordered Captain Hunter.

"Listen, William," my uncle said in an odd voice, "There's something I must tell you about Fairfax—"

"Later," Hunter said again.

I tried once more: "Captain Steele is—"

"Later!" roared Hunter.

My uncle was saying, "Lieutenant Fairfax is—"

"Quiet!" Hunter shouted, in a voice of command that made both of us hush. He then said, "Later we'll have a council of war. But the first thing to do is to get the ship safely to sea!"

Already sails were dropping and filling with the night breeze, and already the *Aurora* was gliding away from the wharf. The moon went behind a cloud. I heard, or imagined I heard, the clatter of hoofs from somewhere ashore. But if it was Steele, or Steele's men, they were too late. The *Aurora* and those who sailed on her were safe.

At least for the moment.

CHAPTER NINE

Council of War

"MEADE WAS STEELE?" Captain Hunter stood in the middle of his great cabin, his mouth opened like that of a hooked fish.

"Aye, and probably still is," said Uncle Patch, sprawled in one of the chairs, his blunt, powerful fingers massaging his forehead.

Hunter clenched both fists. "I had him . . . he was there, right there, across the table from me . . . Jack Steele himself . . . thunder and blast! Why didn't you tell me?"

"Because Davy did not know," said Lieutenant Fairfax from where he sat slumped forward with his head on the captain's table. "None of us knew. I did not, and I saw the man almost every day for near a month."

William Hunter strode back and forth across the length of the cabin like a tiger in a cage. Jessie and I were sitting on his cot, and I was hoping he would forget we were there.

"How could I *not* have known!" Hunter raged. "Why did not I notice? He fit every description of the monster!"

"Calm yourself, now, William. You will worry yourself into an apoplexy!" Uncle Patch snapped, still rubbing his forehead. "Tall and pale, so your description of Steele goes. Well, Meade was tall and pale, but he faded into the background, so he did, save for that white wig that made you overlook every other feature. He made us see just what he wanted us to see, just as you do in your ridiculous pirate costume."

Hunter drew himself up with injured dignity. "It is not the same thing at all."

"It is," chimed in Lieutenant Fairfax in his curiously soft voice. "You parade in your marvelously dramatic pirate garb, so no one will see the naval officer you so obviously are. Captain Steele dresses in drab colors so you would not see the pirate in crimson and red everyone is terrified of." He leaned back into his chair. "Are all seafaring men so theatrical?"

At that last comment, Hunter frowned, and my uncle glared at the young man, who sighed. "I'm not a complete popinjay, Dr. Shea. I may not have recognized the most notorious freebooter north of the Spanish Main, but I do have ears. I have heard Meade speak of Steele's plans. His own plans, though he spoke in the third person. I believe Captain Steele is trying to unite all the Brethren of the Coast into one force, commanded, of course, by himself. I believe he was using the late Monsieur Gille to further that purpose. Monsieur Gille was not truly the sponsor of the pirates—Steele was. Gille was a foolish man whom he worked like a puppet on strings."

"Tortuga Harbor is filled with pirate ships," Hunter mused, while my uncle nodded grimly. "United under one commander, they would be the greatest single force in the West Indies. We must do something."

So for the next several hours, the adults plotted

and planned back and forth, or Hunter and Uncle Patch did, with the occasional comment from Fairfax. His words just seemed to annoy my uncle. Finally, the captain threw up his hands. "There's nothing for it. We can't do this alone. We're going to need help. We're going to need the *Concepción*."

Silence fell in the cabin. Naturally, it was my uncle Patch who found his tongue first. "The *Concepción*?" he asked sarcastically. "D'ye mean a big black Spanish brute of a war galleon with more guns than most ships have men? Commanded by a Don who hates pirates? Like us? That *Concepción* is it, now?"

Hunter nodded, and Uncle Patch exploded. "Oh, for the love of heaven, William, have you taken leave of your wee mind? He'll blow us out of the water as soon as he sees us! And he has reason, for the last time we met you took down his mizzenmast and cost him a prize! We won't be that lucky twice. And even if he does treat with us, you can no more trust a Spaniard to honor a flag of truce than you can an—"

"Englishman?" flared Hunter. I had never seen him so angry.

With a rueful grin, my uncle said softly, "Aye. Or an Irishman who lets his tongue run away now and again."

"Dr. Shea is correct," said Lieutenant Fairfax slowly. "I have heard much about Don Esteban. There is no way Don Esteban will allow the *Aurora* close enough to treat. However, if you come close enough where he can see a flag of truce, you can send me over in a boat and I can appeal to him."

Uncle Patch turned absolutely purple, and I feared for his heart. Why was he getting furious every time the lieutenant made a suggestion? He spluttered, "Of all the harebrained—I forbid it!"

The lieutenant stared at him coldly. "For what reason?"

"Ye know full well!" My uncle swallowed his rage and dropped his voice into a harsh whisper you could still have heard in Port Royal. "Don't push this matter, I warn you. Luck and pluck will take ye only so far."

"What is the matter with you two?" the captain snapped. "This is a brave offer, Patch, bravely made!"

Lieutenant Fairfax smiled, and Uncle Patch

snarled. Jessie murmured, "He's going to tell!"

"Tell what?" I asked, as ignorant as an egg.

"Then it's settled," Fairfax said.

But Hunter shook his head. "No, sir, it is not. If Don Esteban would not listen to a pirate, he surely would not listen to an officer of His Majesty's Royal Navy."

My uncle crossed his arms. "Well?" he asked. "Are you going to answer that?"

For a moment, Fairfax sat silent. Then, with a curious smile at my uncle, he said, "I have heard of Don Esteban, the gallant privateer." His hands worked away at the black ribbon that tied his hair back behind his head. "And while it is true he hates the English as much as he hates pirates, he is said to be most civilized where women are concerned." And he shook his head, and rich chestnut hair flew in all directions.

"Ah, such a gorgeous head and not a brain in it," Jessie muttered behind me. "Now we're in for it."

I didn't say a word because, like Captain Hunter, I was sitting there with my mouth open. The soft lieutenant had disappeared, and in his place—and in his clothes, which were what had so scandalized

Uncle Patch—stood a striking young woman with a very smug smile on her beautiful face. For a change, the first person to speak was the captain.

"You," he said in an accusing voice, "are a woman!"

Uncle Patch creaked with laughter. "Faith, I wondered how long it would be! If you'd stop playacting yourself long enough to take notice of those around you—"

The woman combed her thick hair back from her face with her fingers. "I am afraid that Jessie wasn't the only one who felt it necessary to alter her appearance when the *Venture* was taken. I can't tell you how hard it was to keep up the charade, but the two of us managed."

Hunter turned a beady eye on my uncle. "How long have you known about this, Doctor?"

Uncle Patch sniffed. "I would be no doctor at all, now, if I could not diagnose a patient's gender. How long have I known? Since the first time I clapped eyes on the lieutenant, though she begged me not to break the news to you until she told you first."

The captain took a deep breath and held it for a long time before he let it out. "Madam," he said formally, "I fear you have the advantage of me."

"Forgive my rudeness, sir," she said, bowing prettily from the waist. "I am Miss Helena Fairfax, and I am entirely in your debt."

Uncle Patch, still making the odd creaking sound that was his way of laughing, said, "Now is that your true last name, or is it negotiable?"

"It is Fairfax, Doctor. I am the only daughter of the late Francis Fairfax, Viscount Almsby, and Lady Helena Trevor Fairfax. My brother, Richard, is the present Viscount Almsby. You'd like him. He is an officer, too, but in the army. He falls off his horse now and then, but I imagine you sailors must have occasional seasickness."

"Well," said Hunter. "Of course it's clean out of the question now. You could not possibly negotiate with Don Esteban."

Miss Fairfax drew herself up to her full height, which put the top of her head right under the captain's chin. "Neither you nor I have any choice, Captain Hunter. I know ships, sir. My uncle Vere is a vice-admiral. I know of the pirate armada waiting in Tortuga Harbor. And I know who will command them and what he waits for!"

"What he waits for?" snapped Hunter. "What's that?"

"I know you are brave, sir. Your surgeon has spoken to me of your deeds, and I have seen you in action. But I have seen something you have not and it frightens me more than anything I might have suffered at the Commodore's."

And now I could see the fear in her eyes and even as she set her jaw, her face became pale. "Tell us," my uncle said, quite gently.

With her eyes flashing, Miss Fairfax said, "I have seen the *Red Queen*, Captain Hunter, towering over Shark's *Sultana*, like a castle over a cabin, all over blood and gold. She is what Steele waits for, queen to his king."

"The *Queen* may well be delayed," said Hunter. "Somehow Steele will have to get a message to her. If the messenger was stopped, then perhaps she would not come at all."

"The *Red Queen* will come, sir," said Miss Fairfax definitely. "I have heard the talk, and you may depend upon it. The *Red Queen* will come."

In the deepening silence we all took in what Miss Fairfax had said. The *Red Queen* was the most fearsome ship of war in these seas. If Steele was indeed only waiting for her to sail into Tortuga Harbor—

Well, we were going to need all the help we could get. Even from the *Concepción*.

For the next two days, we prowled the seas to the west of Tortuga, men constantly scanning the horizon for sight of a great black warship with a red and gold flag. Miss Fairfax and Jessie were in residence in Captain Hunter's cabin. Old Phineas Grice, the sailmaker, hauled in bolts of captured silk and satin. He had turned tailor for the time, and was helping Miss Fairfax stitch together a gown or two, for if she was to appeal to Don Esteban, she could hardly do so dressed as a man. I wondered what sort of scarecrow costume Mr. Grice would work up, for he was one of Morgan's crew, a rough old pirate.

Meanwhile, Jessie sat cross-legged on the deck, her sharp tongue tight in the corner of her mouth, sewing scraps of cloth together with tiny, tiny stitches. I had no idea that women's clothing was so complicated.

Late on the second day, the lookout cried out, "A sail!" and pointed to the west at the same time. We crowded to the rail and there she was, at first just the faint flash of white as the lowering sun struck her sails. We altered course, and before long, we saw her hull-up, riding the horizon like a great black crow hovering over the water.

She saw us and changed her own course, coming up fast. When she was close enough, the captain ordered one of the windward guns fired to show that he wanted a peaceful encounter, and had the men haul up the white flag of truce. We all held our breaths until the *Concepción* fired her own gun and hoisted her own white flag.

"Well," muttered Hunter, "at least he won't blow us out of the water without saying a polite hello first."

In the face of my uncle's strong objections, I had been chosen to row Miss Fairfax and Jessie over. Nothing looks less like a boarding party than a twelve-year-old boy, the captain said. Then the doors to the grand cabin opened, and our negotiators stepped out on deck, followed by a beaming sailmaster.

I was impressed. Phineas did good work. Miss Fairfax wore a pale dress of cream-colored silk with all those strange ruffles and tucks quality women seem so fond of. And behind her came Jessie, her head demurely down, and clad in a maid dress that made me almost forget she was, well, Jessie. The men stood around, and a number of them even removed their hats. Captain Hunter came up and bowed to them. Miss Fairfax curtsied, and Jessie bobbed.

"You have the letter I wrote, ma'am?" he asked, sounding as if he had to struggle to speak.

"It is safe, Captain," Miss Fairfax said.

"We had better go, then," said a dry voice. My uncle had come up on deck and stood there with his red hair blowing in the wind.

"Doctor you can't go," said Hunter.

With a face of thunder, Uncle Patch said, "I shall go indeed, sir! You will not dispatch my nephew alone on this errand. I shall remain in the boat while he helps the women onboard, but, by heaven, I shall go."

I watched the captain's face. It was like some actor's in a play—anger, frustration, and then a kind of amusement flitted across it. "Go, then," he finally said, mildly enough.

As we all stood aside so that the ladies could descend into the boat, Jessie swept by me and whispered out of the corner of her mouth, "If you say one word about the way I look, Davy Shea, I shall thump you, I swear I will!" Some things never change.

The sailors helped my uncle clamber down. It was a wonder to me that someone so sure in operating on the human body should be so clumsy in a boat, but there it was. He could not row at all, could not even manage a canoe, and so he sat at the tiller, and I rowed for all I was worth across the space between the ships. Every time I looked over my shoulder, the *Concepción* loomed even larger, towering up out of the sea like a wooden fortress. I tried to count her gun ports and kept getting lost somewhere around forty.

"It's quite large, isn't it?" Jessie asked, her voice shaking.

"Ha!" said my uncle. "You should see her when she is unloading a broadside at you! Easy, Davy, here we are."

There we were indeed, right up against her black

sides, with the Spanish crew staring down at us. They tossed a line, which I made fast to the bow of the little skiff. They had lowered man-ropes to make our climb easier. I gulped and moved aside as Miss Fairfax and Jessie made their way up the ladder to the deck where they were helped onboard. I scurried up after them. No one helped me. I found myself on the deck of the ship that Mr. Jeffers, our chief gunner, had referred to as a Spanish beauty. He wasn't half wrong.

The *Concepción* was much broader than the *Aurora* and her sides twice as thick. The deck swarmed with Spanish sailors. A file of marines stood on the quarterdeck, their long, heavy muskets at the ready. They stared at us as if we were some flight of exotic birds that had landed among them. Everything aboard gleamed with a well-scrubbed look and I realized that, contrary to Mr. Jeffers's opinions on Spanish seamanship, this ship at least was disciplined and ready for anything.

Miss Fairfax swept grandly toward the stern, where a covey of elegantly dressed officers stood, staring down at her from the quarterdeck. One of them stepped forward, and I knew I was looking at

Don Esteban de Reyes, captain of the *Concepción*. Miss Fairfax smiled up at him, all white teeth and wide, wide eyes. She said, "I am Miss Helena Fairfax. Have I the pleasure of addressing Don Esteban de Reyes, captain of this formidable vessel?"

The Spanish captain made a sweeping, deep bow. "I am Don Esteban de Reyes, my lady." He spoke English with a slightly musical, almost lisping accent. I would learn later that his native Spanish was pure Castilian. "You were not what I had expected at all."

He was a short, stocky man, broad in the shoulders and round in the face. Compared with his officers, he was plainly dressed in a black uniform with little decoration. The sword at his side was also plain and undecorated, the leather bindings on the hilt worn smooth from use. Don Esteban was like his ship: broad, probably a bit slow, and very powerful. I remembered what Captain Hunter had once said about the only way to fight the *Concepción*—hit her fast, hit her hard, and then run like the devil. I thought the same could be said for her captain. He was smiling, but the smile left his eyes cold and calculating.

Miss Fairfax produced a folded white paper. "I come bearing a message from Captain William Hunter, master of the *Aurora*, with whom I believe you are familiar?"

Gravely, Don Esteban nodded. "Yes, I am most familiar with the *Aurora*. Thank you for informing me of her captain's name." He spoke over his shoulder to his officers in Spanish, and I could understand only the strangely pronounced "Huntair." Don Esteban turned back, the smile still on his face. "And how did so obviously a lady as yourself come to be on the ship of such a man?"

Miss Fairfax held her chin up. "Captain Hunter did me the favor of rescuing my maid and me from the notorious pirate king, Jack Steele!"

The smile vanished from the Spaniard's face, leaving it as blank as a slate wiped clean. He swept over us with a black gaze that made me flinch. "So?" he asked in a voice of soft menace. "Steele, is it?"

Miss Fairfax held out the note. "Though he may be a pirate, Captain Hunter has no love for Jack Steele. His plans are a threat to anyone who sails the seas."

Don Esteban stared at the paper but did not

move to take it. "And what, dear lady, has this to do with me?"

"Captain Hunter has two requests, sir. One, that you convey my maid and me to the safety of Port Royal. Second, he asks that you consider a truce and an alliance."

At last Don Esteban took the note from her. The Spanish captain carefully broke the wax and opened the folded paper. His eyes moved back and forth. Finally, he folded it again, and slowly the smile returned to his face. "The Spanish is passable. Surprising in an English. An interesting proposal, well thought out. But why should I believe such a man?"

"Captain Hunter is a man of his word!" I heard a voice ring out. To my horror, I recognized it as my own. Don Esteban did not even look at me. His eyes stayed locked on Miss Fairfax's.

"I do not take the word of a pirate, Miss Fairfax. Give me yours."

She raised an eyebrow. I had never seen anyone act so cool in such a situation. "Sir?"

Captain Reyes spread his hands. "It is simple. Give me your word as an English lady that what the captain writes here is true and I will believe it." The smile stayed, but his voice dropped until only we could hear it. "But swear me false and I assure you the *Aurora* will go straight to the bottom, and you shall see her sink."

Miss Fairfax was as pale as an ivory statue, but her back was straight and her voice steady as she said, "I swear upon my honor that both Captain Hunter and his plan are true."

He stared at her for a moment longer and then nodded. "Very well."

Behind me Jessie gave a shuddering gasp of relief, and I remembered to breathe myself.

We had struck a deal with the devil we didn't know to fight the devil we did.

And only time would tell if he would play true with us.

CHAPTER TEN

The Brig

MY UNCLE AND I made the best of our way
back to the *Aurora*, leaving Miss Fairfax behind on
the *Concepción*. To tell the truth, I was more than a
little afraid as we moved away from the big Spanish
ship, for she had cannons enough to sink us without a second thought. I hoped that Miss Fairfax
was right in her estimation of Don Esteban, and
that he would be gallant enough to stand by our
truce.

Three miles of open sea in a small boat is no easy
trip on a day when the sea is choppy, and so right
glad I was when we hauled up alongside of the
Aurora again. I was first from the boat, and sprang

up the side ladder like a good 'un. My uncle followed more clumsily, and we found the captain waiting for us. I could not help thinking just then how six months at sea had changed me. There had been a time when climbing easily up the side of even so moderate a ship as the *Aurora* would have been beyond me, as it still was beyond my poor uncle. But now I went up with no more thought than I would have given to running upstairs at Mr. Horne's house in Bristol, where I had been brought up.

"What's the word?" Hunter asked anxiously as soon as my feet hit the deck.

"He says he is willing to hold his fire," I reported. "He would commit to no more."

Uncle Patch gazed with moody eyes across the three miles of sea at the big Spaniard. "Faith, I wish we had more to go on than the word of a Don. You know, William, the thought strikes me that Don Esteban would be mighty pleased to join us in sinking Jack Steele, and then turn his guns upon us."

"You are not alone in your thought," said Hunter cheerfully. "However, that must bide the touch. For now our concern is to find some way of breaking up Steele's armada, before the *Red Queen* can come to lead them. I wish we knew what his target is. Tortuga itself? Not impossible, not with so many of the old Brethren of the Coast ready to throw in their lots with him. You might know that the British took the island from the Spanish in one day, fifty years ago or so. Or might Steele be thinking of Port Royal? Jamaica, now, would be a fat prize, and the key to it is Port Royal."

"Or might he be thinking of sailing across the sea and up the Thames, to throw the king into the Tower and declare himself monarch of England?" my uncle said sarcastically. "What we do not know, we do not, and there's an end to it."

Hunter put his hands behind him and stared out to sea. "Not quite, Doctor. For if Steele plans to make an assault on Tortuga, we must move quickly. Aye, it would be a master blow, at that. To put abroad the word that he is going after the English, or the Spanish, and to mass an armada in Tortuga Harbor, and then turn his guns on the French— why, 'twould be a deed that people would remember for an age or more."

"The way they remember how Morgan butchered the people at Port Principe, or at Portobello," agreed Uncle Patch. "A rogue's fame, not an honest man's. Though why you even worry about what happens to the French is beyond me."

"I worry," returned the captain, "because if Steele once gets snug into Tortuga, it will be well-nigh impossible to pry him out again. You saw the harbor. With the fort properly manned, it's secure against a navy. It is an Acropolis, a Masada. Give Steele a base of his own, and he will make himself the king of the West Indies, if not the king of England."

"Well, well," muttered Uncle Patch, "you may be right. But I see no way at all of fighting off the ships anchored in Tortuga Harbor. We may have the big Spaniard to help us, and they may be mostly a collection of sloops and brigs, but, faith, they outnumber us dozens to one."

"I am thinking of that too," said Captain Hunter.

And so, I believe, was every man aboard the *Aurora*.

Like a mouse trying to be friends with a cat, we came close enough to the *Concepción* to exchange signals. Don Esteban agreed to meet us off the east coast of Tortuga in a week's time. We parted with that, he sailing to the southeast, we to the southwest. Seeing the Spanish ship drop below the horizon gave me a strange feeling. I did not know when or even whether I would see Jessie again. She had not exactly been my best friend back in Port Royal, but we had spent time talking, with me teaching her to read and all. I worried about what might happen to her, and I hoped that no ill would come to her. Though as to that, she was more the type of person who happened to others than the one who had things happen to her.

A night passed, and then early the next morning the lookout spied a sail north of us. "She's tearing along like smoke and oakum!" he called down to the deck.

Hunter climbed to the masthead and hung there in the shrouds with his best telescope clapped to his eye. "A brig," he reported after studying the stranger. "And in a great hurry, with all sails spread alow and aloft. I wonder, now. Sailmaker!"

Mr. Grice, the old pirate who took care of the *Aurora*'s sails, came up, quick as a cricket. "Aye, sir?"

Hunter had swung down a backstay and lighted on the deck as nimbly as a cat. "D'you know Steele's flag?" he demanded.

Phineas Grice must have been nearly seventy, a short, bowed little man with a sharp chin and a deep, suspicious squint. His hair was long and white, and he never exactly had a beard and was never clean-shaven. Now he rubbed a hand over his bristles, making a sound like sandpaper. "Red flag, in course, with a skull and crossed swords. His sailing mates fly the same, but in black."

"Could you run a black one up in, say, an hour?"

"Easy enough done," said the sailmaker. He grinned a toothless grin. "False colors is it, Cap'n?"

"A ruse of war," Hunter said with a wink. "Hop to it!"

Grice hurried away. Uncle Patch came up onto the deck, quite early, for him, for it was only four bells in the morning watch. "What's Grice so happy about?" he asked. "Faith, he looks like the shark that ate the admiral."

"Good morning, Doctor," Hunter said. "In rather more than three glasses, we are going to cross the bow of a brig. It has the look of the *Viper*, and if it is that vessel, why, I want to have a word with her captain. Sam Dobbs has been an errand boy for Jack Steele many and many a time, and I just wonder if he's sailing for Tortuga with news for Steele, or to get orders from him."

My uncle yawned and stretched. "And you think he'll tell you if you ask nicely? 'Tis a touching faith you have in human nature, to be sure, William."

"We may have to ask less than nicely," Hunter told him, and the devil another word would he say.

Three glasses is an hour and a half, the glasses being the sand glasses we used to keep time during the watches. When one ran out, someone would turn it and sing, "Ring the bell!" The first bell was a half hour into the watch, two bells one hour, three bells an hour and a half, and so on, all the way to eight bells, when the watch ended and the whole count started over again. I swear, though, that the sand never ran so slowly as it did that day.

Mr. Grice was back well before the brig had come close, and he displayed his handiwork proudly. He had whipped up a Jolly Roger much like ours, except that the skull had an evil leer. Its eye sockets were a brilliant red—satin, carefully sewn in. Beneath it, instead of crossed bones, were two crossed cutlasses, in white, with yellow hilts. And though rough stitching might have done for this job, Grice had been as careful as a tailor. Captain Hunter held up the flag and nodded his satisfaction. "A first-class job, Mr. Grice. Now let's see whether we can beguile a pirate."

He had the flag run right up to the masthead, and then he ordered signals: "Message aboard from Steele."

"There," he said, when all flags were flying. "If the brig is what I think she is, that ought to fetch her. If she is honest, then she'll sheer off as soon as she can make out the Jolly Roger. We shall see shortly."

The brig was four miles off, then three, then two. And then she altered her course. She was sailing for us. Our path was rapidly converging with hers. "Good," Hunter pronounced. "Mr. Adams! I'll need thirty men. Pick some with level heads who know how to keep quiet. Here's what we shall do. . . ."

My uncle came over to listen, and even he, the arch-plotter himself, seemed grudgingly impressed.

"I'll be at my post in the sick berth," he declared when Hunter finished, "just in case your plan miscarries and we have to pluck lead out of some of our men."

I knew that meant he expected me to be there too. But Hunter laughed at his concerns. "If I handle this right, you needn't worry," he assured my uncle. "Let us try diplomacy before we fly to the weapons."

"Faith, you're like Saul on the road to Damascus," growled my uncle. "A convert, so you are! But I'll at least lay out my instruments, just in case."

When the brig was less than half a mile away, it fired a gun on the side opposite us. Hunter glanced at Mr. Warburton, the helmsman. "Is it the same as with honest ships?" he asked.

Warburton spat to leeward. "Give 'er a gun to windward," he said shortly. "Then if she don't suspect aught, she'll dip her flag."

Hunter gave the order, and Mr. Adams fired one of the forward cannons, not taking time to unload the ball. It skipped on the sea six times, then sank. Immediately the brig lowered its own flag, an innocent-looking one that proclaimed her to be a Dutch merchant, and hove to.

"Mr. Adams, you know what to do," said Mr. Hunter. "Cox'n, my barge."

Abel Tate was the captain's coxswain. It was his job to take charge of the boat whenever the captain was leaving the ship. He and six crewmen lowered away the gig, and Captain Hunter stepped over the side and climbed down to it. Seeing that my uncle was not watching, I followed close behind and dropped into the stern of the boat an instant after Hunter.

"Davy!" the captain exclaimed in surprise. Then he grinned. "Well, well, the *Viper* won't expect any uproar from us if we even have the cabin boy aboard, will he?"

"No, sir," I said, though that had not even occurred to me.

"Row us over, Mr. Tate," Hunter said. He had the wolfish look that meant he anticipated action of some sort.

The *Viper* was a brig, a two-masted vessel with square sails on both masts. This one carried sixteen guns, and a crowd of sailors came to the rails to stare at us as we pulled over. Tate brought the gig up to the side of the brig, and Hunter climbed up, with me at his heels. Behind us, the *Aurora*, with only her jib set, drifted closer.

"You come from the *Red Queen*?" Hunter asked.

The captain of the brig, for such I supposed him, stepped forward with a frown. He was an unshaven man of thirty or so, with greasy black hair and a scar right across his face, left cheek to right, slanting across a broken nose. "Who th' devil are ye?" he demanded.

"I come from Steele," snapped Hunter. "Plans have changed."

There were perhaps thirty men on the deck of the brig. They stared at us with muttering hostility. "Who are ye?" demanded the brig's captain again. "What d'ye mean, 'changed'?"

Hunter pushed past him, toward the stern. He climbed the few steps to the low quarterdeck and walked past the helmsman at the tiller, who gawked at him. "I can't say much for your lookout," Hunter thundered. "You didn't see what was following you?"

"Following us?"

Hunter pointed off to the north. "Hull-down, but you can catch the flash of those topsails! Steele won't be happy when he sees what you've dragged down with you!"

That was too much for the crew. Pretty nearly every one of them rushed back to the stern, and there were angry questions: "What is it?" "Where away?" "Not that cursed Spaniard, is it?"

"I see nothing," declared the pirate captain.

Hunter made a deep growl of disgust. "North by northeast, and bear a point east!" he yelled. "Are you blind?"

By now they were all shading their eyes with their hands. I think I was the only one who saw Hunter gesture with his left hand for me to back away. I did, back to the ladder. The longboat from the *Aurora* had just pulled up, and ten men were poised to spring up for the brig's rail.

"There!" Hunter said with a villainous curse. He drew his cutlass and pointed northward at the empty sea. "What are you using for eyes?" I see her plain!"

"What do you see?" demanded the pirate.

Hunter turned on him with a grin. "I see a captain

and crew who are about to lose their brig! Board 'em, men!"

With horrible cries, the *Auroras* made their leap, ten, and ten more, and ten after that. The *Vipers* were taken completely by surprise. One or two of them pulled their weapons, but Hunter had already placed his point against their captain's chest. "Do you surrender?"

With a terrible curse and a glare, the pirate captain snarled, "Aye! But Steele will cut out your living guts for this!"

"If he gets the chance," Hunter agreed smoothly. "Mr. Adams, take possession!"

Within an hour, the *Viper* was ours, and her own crew were bobbing about in two overfull boats. Hunter left them with food and water, and the cheerful news that a hundred mile's row would bring them to safety, on a Spanish island. He, Tate, and I went back to the *Aurora*, along with most of the boarders, leaving behind just a skeleton crew of ten to sail her and to see what she had worth our attention.

That turned out to be two things. The first

interested Morgan's men prodigiously, for the *Viper* carried six chests with sixty thousand pieces of eight in them, all told. "The wages of sin, I fancy," Hunter said when Mr. Adams brought the news. "Let the men know."

Indeed they knew, and everyone wore sharkish grins. Though we were a hired vessel, not truly a pirate ship, Hunter's letter of marque specified that he could reward the crew out of his prizes. We had not done so badly up until that time, but now the capture of the *Viper* meant that every man of the crew was at least a hundred pounds richer. I had the mere quarter of a share, and even so, my part would run to thirty pounds or more. It was more money than I had ever seen at one time in my life, and almost more than I could hope to spend in a year!

But the second prize, for Hunter, was the better one. In the captain's cabin of the *Viper* Mr. Adams found a few sheets of parchment, with signals and notes upon them. Hunter studied them with a satisfied gleam in his eyes. "Now we know their secret signals," he said. "According to this, the *Red Queen* will stand off and on until she gets word from Steele to come to the harbor—her cruising area's not named, though, worse luck. But the signal list gives us something to plan with!"

I did not know precisely what the plan was, for my uncle was not pleased with my slipping away with Hunter, and he banished me from the cabin for the next several days. We made our rendezvous with the *Concepción*, and Hunter exchanged a flurry of signals with Don Esteban. I could not read them, and no one would tell me what they said, though I complained bitterly to anyone who would stand still long enough to listen.

"The wind is just right," pronounced Hunter when Don Esteban had evidently agreed to whatever it was we were about to do. "It will be tricky, but we should be able to get in, spin about, and get out again before they know what we're up to."

Now the *Viper* had just six men aboard her, with Mr. Adams in command. At a signal from Hunter, both she and the *Aurora* hoisted sails and made for Tortuga Harbor, the *Aurora* in the lead, but both vessels close-hauled to the wind. We made splendid time. The white water flew from our bows in a rush. Before long, we entered the harbor, small craft scattering from our headlong, mad dash. "Now!" Hunter shouted, and a flutter of signal flags went up.

"What's he saying?" I asked my uncle, without much hope.

"Faith, little do I know of the language of flags," he returned sharply, "but as I understand it, William is telling all the pirate ships in the harbor that a Spanish ship of the line is chasing us and the *Viper*."

Then, from the channel far behind us, came a sound like distant thunder. It was the booming of the *Concepción*'s cannons.

Hunter was gazing astern, muttering, "Come on, Adams, come on . . . good man!"

The *Viper* had drawn abreast of us. I saw the six men dash along the rail, stooping at six of the guns. And the next instant, the side of the brig vanished as all six guns roared at once!

"They're firing on us!" I yelped.

"With powder, not with shot," my uncle said coolly. "Watch now!"

"Hoist the second signal!" roared Hunter. "Man the guns!"

The six men aboard the *Viper* had dived into the

harbor, and Abel Tate was throwing a line over the rail. As soon as they were clear of the brig, Hunter ordered, "Fire! Aim true!"

Our cannon crews bent over their pieces, and we sent a broadside booming over the water—clean missing the *Viper*, only yards from our side. But the evenly grouped balls flew past the brig and smashed into the Hornet, a light pirate frigate of twenty guns.

I turned to my uncle. With a frosty smile, he said, "With any luck, the *Hornet* will think the *Viper* just fired on her. And Hunter is signaling *Treason! Tell Steele!* Let them think that the *Viper*'s crew has sold them out."

Gray, soaked, swung aboard, together with the rest of his prize crew. The *Hornet*'s gunners were scrambling to run out their cannons. Smoke was pouring from the *Viper*'s stern.

"Is she well alight, Mr. Adams?" Hunter asked.

"Aye, sir!" returned our lieutenant. "Lord, I hate a fire ship!"

"So does every sailor, even pirates," said Hunter. "Put her about! They're going to catch on in seconds, and then they're going to come chasing us!"

The unmanned *Viper* suddenly blossomed into flame and smoke. She sailed smack into a sloop, tangled with its rigging, and the two slewed around, fouling the rigging of a barque. By then we had put the *Aurora* about.

The harbor was behind us now, and the *Viper* almost leaped from the water with a shattering explosion. Flaming timbers flew tumbling through the air, and the sloop entangled with the wreck began to blaze. A second explosion burst out, sending billows of thick smoke curdling on the wind.

"That'll be the gunpowder," Abel Tate observed mildly. "Hah! They're firin' at each other! A fine old dance the cap'n's going to lead them!"

Uncle Patch put his hand on my shoulder. "Let's go downstairs," he said.

"Belowdecks," Tate corrected him automatically.

"To our place," my uncle said firmly. "To the sick berth."

And faith, at that moment his face looked more dangerous than all the pirate ships in the harbor, and so I dared do nothing other than follow him down, meek as a lamb.

CHAPTER ELEVEN

The Pirate Armada

DESPITE MY UNCLE'S orders, I kept darting up onto the deck to catch glimpses of what was going on. Tortuga Harbor was now a churning mass of ships and flame. When the *Viper* exploded, she had spread burning timbers and canvas over everything. Other ships had caught fire, and bits of the debris had landed on some of the ramshackle warehouses that lined the wharves. The first cherry-red flames were just now starting to lick up from their palmetto-thatched roofs.

"Run up more of the flags, Mr. Adams!" Captain Hunter roared, waving his cutlass in the air and looking every inch a pirate captain. Mr. Adams nodded and rushed to send up more signal flags. I was to learn later that they repeated the same message in different words: *Treason. Treason. Beware. Beware. Trust no one.*

Screams and cries of rage echoed around us, even louder than the crack and roar of the flames and the booms of cannons. Sloops and brigs were struggling to cast themselves off and set sail, to escape the harbor and the burning ships that multiplied even as we looked. The *Aurora* let loose another broadside into the billowing clouds of smoke that just moments before had been the *Viper*. Since that doughty little brig had all but disappeared beneath the water, the shot sailed right through the smoke and crashed into the already damaged *Hornet* and the warehouses beyond. Timbers and roofing blew up into the air like ugly fireworks. The *Hornet*, her sails burning to floating black ash, began to sink by the stern, her crew finally giving up their useless guns and scrambling to reach the wharf. I would have expected them to throw themselves into the harbor and escape that way, but I had learned in my time at sea that most sailors—pirate or otherwise—cannot swim.

We were coming about now to begin our run out of the harbor, bringing the wind on our starboard quarter. We were ready to make the dash for safety when out of the smoke and flames came the *Fury*, Captain John Barrel's sloop with whom we had entered Tortuga Harbor five weeks past. That worthy himself stood on her railing, balanced on his good leg, his left arm wrapped securely around a line. He raised a speaking trumpet to his lips and called out, "Ahoy, the *Aurora*! Ahoy, Captain Hunter! What in all the black blazes is going on?"

Mr. Adams handed Captain Hunter his own speaking trumpet, and he called back. "Treachery, Captain Barrel! Treachery most foul!"

"Why did you fire into one of Steele's vessels?" bawled Barrel.

The captain answered him in a voice that must have carried across the harbor: "*Viper* was sailing under false colors, Captain Barrel! She was nothing but a Judas-goat for the bloody Dons! Did you not see how she opened up on us with no warning?"

"Aye, we saw that!" returned Barrel with an oath. "Sam Dobbs always was a hound!"

"Beware traitors among us, Captain Barrel!"

called Captain Hunter. "Who knows how many the Dons have bought! Follow us out and we may escape yet!"

"Lead on—we'll follow!" Barrel leaped from the railing and landed with a thud on the *Fury*'s deck. "Stand fast, ye sea dogs, to yer stations, and follow the *Aurora*!"

We slipped past the heavily armed sloop, flags flying and guns blazing. I could almost hear the words racing from pirate ship to pirate ship. Treachery, treason, betrayal. In the confusion, ships were running foul of each other, some burning, some not. And ship after ship ran out her guns and opened fire on anything in her path. Captain Hunter had said that would happen. Let the suspicion loose and every man would remember the injuries he had suffered from every other man. They'd see it as a chance to settle old scores and destroy traitors at the same time.

The fires ashore were spreading. The warehouses we had hit while firing on the fire ship were filled with refitting supplies, cordage and timber and pitch and, heaven help us all, powder and shot. I could see scurrying figures raising up buckets of water from the harbor and hurling them on the flames. One of the warehouses erupted in a huge gout of boiling orange flame and black smoke.

"It's working, Uncle Patch!" I cried, staring out at the wreckage and flames.

"'Tis working for the now, boy," my uncle snarled, his head and shoulders sticking up through the hatch. "But *now* isn't *forever*, and Lucifer laughs at the hopeful! Come below, now, and help me prepare!"

So I ran down again to help him. Still, even in the sick berth I could glimpse the battle, through the wind-port that my uncle had caused to be cut in the side during the frigate's refitting. It was not much of a window, but it was enough to give me a prospect of what was happening outside. Suddenly a new booming thundered out over the lesser roars from the ships. Huge fountains of water leaped into the air. It took me a second to realize what had happened, and then I cried out, "Uncle! The great guns in the fort are firing!"

"And who do they think they're firing at, I wonder?" Uncle Patch said with a snort. "As if the blessed fools could tell friend from foe down here!"

Almost at the moment he said that, a second warehouse exploded, sending a vast fireball up into the sky. Now ships were running afoul of one another, tangling their lines and spars together until they were hopelessly bound together. Still, a number of them had managed to get underway and fall in behind us and the *Fury*. Others continued to savage one another, paying off past injuries. My eyes began to ache from the horror of it all.

When my uncle's instruments were laid out and ready, he grudgingly told me I might go on deck, until casualties began to come down. I got there just as we were passing the arms of the harbor, heading out to the open sea and what waited there for us.

And that was the Spanish war galleon *Concepción*.

The faster ships, the sloops and such like, had overtaken and passed us in their race to escape Tortuga. They were the first to come under the guns of the big Spaniard. How could they have missed her? She was there with all her sails set, coming down on us like a white stormcloud low on the sea. Her scarlet and gold banner caught the sunlight like silken flames and I shuddered at the sight of her.

"Lord, Uncle Patch!" I cried as my uncle came up the ladder onto the deck. "Look at her come!"

"Aye," he said, shading his eyes. "Even an elephant will move like a tiger if you give it enough of a start!"

The lead ships, finally sensing their danger, began to turn to leeward, but the war galleon blocked their escape. Then as she sailed between a brig and a sloop, her guns cut loose, both broadsides at the same time. Everywhere white smoke billowed across the water. Then the *Concepción* shouldered her way through, leaving behind her a shattered wreck on one side and mere debris on the other.

"Find the Captain," my uncle shouted over the noise. "Tell that English madman that I'm ready for the wounded. Send 'em down as they fall!" And he dropped belowdecks again.

In a flash, I was up the ladder and onto the quarterdeck. Clouds of acrid gun smoke broke across us, and the *Concepción* let loose another deafening broadside. Our own gunners huddled around their guns, matches and swabs, powder and shot at the ready. Over the rumble and roar I heard my gunner friend, Mr. Jeffers, yell at one of his crew, "Now that's what I call gunnery! Slow, but oh, how accurate!"

I scampered over to where Captain Hunter stood in his green coat and pirate hat. I stammered out my uncle's message and got a distracted nod for my troubles. The captain had other things on his mind.

"Now we will see what a Spaniard's word means," he whispered through clenched teeth. "Bring her about, Mr. Adams, if you please. Come sunset or sunrise, we'll give them a show!"

The *Aurora* began to close on the *Concepción*. In the distance I fancied I could hear Captain Barrel roaring. This was going to be the trickiest part of the whole plan. The next moment was going to decide whether or not we joined the *Viper* and her burning sisters on the bottom of the sea.

"Steady, Mr. Jeffers, steady," Captain Hunter said, slowly raising his cutlass up in the air. All eyes were on him as we closed on the great black war galleon, and I remembered the first time we had met her. The same tall black sides began to tower over us, the multiple gunports gaping wide. I could see the white-clad Spanish gunners crouched over their massive twenty-four-pounders, matches glowing in their hands. For the longest moment we all seemed to stare at one another. Then the signal came.

"Fire and drop!" the captain roared. Men fell to the deck as the gunners applied matches to touch holes. The *Aurora* shuddered as our starboard battery all fired at once. At the same time, the *Concepción*'s two decks opened up in a thunderous blast of flame and sulfuric smoke. Cannon shot whistled over our heads, ripping holes in the lower sails and parting lines. At the same time, I could hear the almost meaty thump of our own shot hitting those great walls.

"'Tis a waste, 'tis a terrible waste!" cried Mr. Jeffers. "Full charges o' powder would hull her!"

"Aye," cried the Captain back at him. "And full powder and shot from that behemoth would have sunk us! Half powder again, Mr. Jeffers, if you please!" As we play-acted with the *Concepción*, she was also engaging the pirate fleet that was trying to fight its way past us.

"Follow the *Aurora*, ya scurvy dogs! Hammer the Spaniard!" Even over the battle, I could hear John Barrel's bull roar. The *Fury* closed in, firing her cannons as she came. Not playacting, she managed to blast some of the gilt off the war galleon's high stern, and a cheer went up. Then the *Concepción* boomed back, and the *Fury* disappeared in a cloud of smoke and flying splinters.

"My eyes, but the old man is a brave one!" Hunter shouted. His cutlass came down, and once again we let loose a broadside, and once again the *Concepción* fired back. More holes appeared in our sails, and a section of the forecastle rail exploded into splinters. At that exact moment, the lower spar on the foremast came crashing down. It was impressive if you didn't know two of our own sailors had cut it loose.

"Two broadsides! No more, lads—that's all I bargained for in my note to the Don!" Hunter swung his cutlass, and we heeled away from our supposed foe. Behind us rolled the thunder of another ragged cannonade, and both the captain and I turned. There, limping out of the smoke and ruin, came the *Fury*, sails holed and hull splintered. But she still had a few guns that worked and she was firing them for all she was worth. And Captain John Barrel still stood on what was left of her deck, blackened by soot and gunpowder and roaring like a madman.

"Keep firing, ye lubbers! Follow the *Aurora* and to blazes with the bloody Dons!" Behind him, another brig was settling fast, but two other crippled sloops began to follow his lead.

We began to pull away to the northwest, faster and faster on a quartering wind, with our small fleet of stragglers behind us. The *Concepción* moved among the rest like an angry terrier among rats. Her guns boomed again and again, and the times between cannonades grew shorter and shorter. Mr. Jeffers nodded approval of Don Esteban's broadsides now that they were no longer directed at us. I could see his opinion of Spanish gunners—or at least these Spanish gunners—improving by the minute.

But even the greatest terrier can be outnumbered by rats. Although ships were sinking all about the *Concepción*, the cannonballs that had pounded into her began to take their toll. A lucky or well-aimed shot brought down her foretopgallantmast. Seeing her crippled, the remaining pirate ships began to haul away to the west, leaving their shattered sisters to founder and burn around their destroyer. For his part, Don Esteban seemed to sense that the day was his and that he need seek no further glory. The *Concepción* turned slowly, delivering another broadside at the fleeing pirates, and then caught the breeze and stood away, south by southwest, with the wind almost on her stern, making for the Windward Passage. More cannon fire broke out. The pirate crews, still unsure of each other, tended to blaze away at any craft that ventured too close.

Mindless of the risk, I stood at the taffrail staring backward as the paths of the vessels diverged and the remnants of battle fell behind us. Of all of us aboard the *Aurora*, I was the only one to see the sleek red galley pull away, leading a string of survivors behind her. The oars flashed, and a red silk flag with a laughing skull fluttered from her mast. For just a second I thought I saw a flash of white that might have been a long white wig. Then she was hidden in the smoke, my view further blocked by the fleeing vessels around her.

But I could guess where she was going and what great crimson ship she was to meet up with out there on the darkening seas. I had met the king of the pirates. I had no wish to meet his *Red Queen*, for if she had arrived beforehand, even with the *Concepción*, the battle would have been in doubt.

And then my uncle was bawling for me. We had some injuries to attend to—nothing serious, but he needed my help. So I turned away from the rail.

Farewell, Captain Steele, I thought, until we meet again.

CHAPTER TWELVE

The Anchorage

HOW CAPTAIN BARREL managed it, I do not to this day know. Somehow he bullied and cursed, threatened and pleaded, and his crew kept the *Fury* limping along, low in the water and threatening to sink at every third wave. My uncle and I went across several times to treat the wounded. Six of them died, and over the side went their bodies, with not so much as a prayer or a moment of silence.

When the water was swishing ankle-deep in the captain's cabin, my uncle whistled and said privately to Barrel, "You ought to bring your men across as soon as may be. She cannot swim another day."

"Swim or sink," the old buccaneer said firmly, "I

stay with the *Fury*, and so do the hands!" And he snorted so fiercely that I heartily believe not one of his sailors would have chosen to leave his vessel.

Even Captain Hunter admired the man. "By heaven, he has pluck," he declared the next day, when we were scarcely seventy miles along and the poor *Fury* was wallowing like a dying whale. "Look how they pump! I wonder his men can even stand after so much effort."

In the glittering sunlight, we could see jets of water shooting from the scuppers of the *Fury*. Captain Barrel himself was at the handles of the pump, and when another man relieved him at the end of his hour, he leaped to the bow of the *Fury* and gave us a cheerful wave.

That afternoon, the lookout sighted land, and as we drew near to it, Captain Hunter looked pleased. "It's Cruzado," he said. "Hardly more than a fly-speck on the ocean, and there's no fresh water there but what falls from the sky, but it has a kind of anchorage."

Cruzado was one of the more southerly Bahamas, entirely different from the mountainous Tortuga or Hispaniola. It rose very gently from the sea, and no spot on it could be much more than ten feet above high tide. Low and green it was, and at first sight quite deserted. But as we came in from the southwest, I could see a scattering of buildings, leaning crazily left and right and gray with weathering. Hunter conned us in to a sort of harbor, a half-circular bite out of the shore. Some men on the land glanced our way, but paid us little attention.

Boddin laughed, a deep musical sound. He was one of the twenty-odd former slaves in our crew, who all preferred a free but danger-filled life on the open sea to security and chains ashore. "The cap'n's a fine navigator," he said to me. "An' he found this place not one minute too soon for the *Fury*."

With all the speed she could muster, and that was no more than a fast walking pace, the *Fury* ran straight past us, up to the shelving shore, and grounded with a sandy sigh on the beach. She tilted to the left and came to rest, and from her worn-out crew I heard a weary cheer.

You would think that after all that, after the sea battle and the desperate run to Cruzado, Barrel would have rested, and let his men rest. But no— before half an hour had passed, her boats were busily ferrying her cargo ashore, lightening her so that later she could be hauled up and careened. Nor did the pumps stop working the whole time.

Indeed, it was three days before Barrel at last was able to see his craft high and dry. If the *Aurora* had borne an ugly hole from cannon fire, the *Fury* was all but a wreck. Her timbers were splintered and splayed, and amidships, as Abel Tate observed with a whistle, "She 'ad bloomed like a flower," letting the sea in and almost sending herself to the bottom.

But Barrel cheerfully swore at the sight and set his carpenter to putting everything back to rights. The men ashore, I had learned, were pirates to a man. Desperate men they were, I have no doubt, and at sea as wicked as you would hope to meet this side of perdition. But Barrel was well liked among them, and they cheerfully agreed to sell him timber and other necessaries on credit.

Barrel came aboard the *Aurora* on the evening of the third day. Up close, I could see how exhausted the man was, and how his hands were cruelly blistered. "Well, well, Doctor," he said with a gaptoothed grin as my uncle met him on deck. "And so

I'm not like to lose more o' my men, d'ye think?"

With a grudging smile, my uncle replied, "By the Powers, Captain Barrel, I do not think a man Jack of your crew would dare to die without your permission."

Barrel threw his great head back and boomed out a laugh. Then he said, "I hear that Cap'n Hunter don't mean to tarry long, so I've come to give him my thanks and to take leave of him."

"Come along," said my uncle, leading the way to the cabin. "I'm sure it's pleased he'll be to have a word with you."

Captain Hunter did look pleased, and he offered Captain Barrel something wet. "I'd not say no to that," Barrel told him. "It's fair parched I am, and that's no lie." I brought out some brandy, and I stood in the corner as Hunter and Barrel drank a toast to the Brethren of the Coast—"them that's above hatches, and them that's shaken the devil's hand," as Barrel put it.

After a second glass, Barrel wiped his mouth on his sleeve and shook his head. "Curse that *Viper* and her fool of a captain," he muttered. "I've studied and studied on it, and 'tis plain what happened.

That 'ere *Concepción* snapped her up an' turned her into a fire ship." He shook his head. "It fair broke up whatever Jack Steele was plannin', ye may lay to that. But he'll be back."

"It's hard to kill a man like Steele," Hunter agreed.

"Aye," agreed Barrel. He got up. "Well, fair winds to ye."

"Here," Hunter said, tossing a leather sack across the table. It landed with the clink of coin.

Barrel picked it up and dumped at least a dozen gold coins into his palm, not even a tenth of what the bag held. "Here. What is this?"

Hunter shrugged. "You're down on your luck. But you won't be always, and when our wakes cross again, I might need help from you. Take it and welcome, for we've been prosperous this voyage."

Barrel shook with laughter. "That's handsome, so it is! And I'll not turn it down, neither. Ye know, Steele will be lookin' for new captains now, what with the wicked wreck that old Spaniard made o' his fleet. I'll put in a word for ye, so I will, for ye've treated me an' my crew fair."

"I would like that," Hunter said.

Soon Barrel left us, and we weighed anchor with the evening tide. As we glided away from the low, green island of Cruzado, I stood on deck looking back. Night was gathering in the eastern sky, and already Venus hung there low and brilliant as a signal lamp.

We were fairly at sea before Hunter and my uncle sat down to supper in the cabin. Hunter told me to sit too, and to share their meal. As he served us, he gave my uncle a quizzical glance. "Why so glum, Doctor?"

Uncle Patch sighed. "I thought I had saved Captain Brixton," he said. "Me with my sinful pride and my sneaking schemes! He was a brave man, for all that he was English."

"Thank you," Hunter said with a twisted smile.

My uncle waved a hand. "Not all of you are ranting, raving lunatics," he said. "But poor Brixton, now—I dearly hope that he did not babble of us and our mission before someone cut his throat."

"I knew him well," Hunter said quietly. "I cannot see him spilling our secrets. Not even if he were not in his perfect mind."

Uncle Patch nodded gloomily. "Then there's this,

too: Brixton was one of the very few men who knew that we are not truly pirates. I feel as if we've lost a lifeline with him gone."

Hunter smiled. "Come, it isn't so bleak. Sir Henry Morgan knows what we are, and he's safe in Port Royal, or at his plantation in Port Maria. And as far as that goes, King James himself knows about us, for it was his hand that signed our commission. As long as our letter of marque is safe in the cabin here, we need not fear the hangman. You surprise me, Doctor. I thought the Irish were braver than that."

Uncle Patch said quietly, "'Twas not for myself that I was concerned."

He did not look at me, but I caught his meaning. My uncle might seem big and bold, and he might give me the sharp edge of his tongue. But for all that, we were family. Somehow I knew that if it came to that, he would lay down his life to save mine. As I write this now, I wish that I had found words to tell him so. I don't know, though. He probably would have snarled, "Now ye're being a sentimental Irishman. Hush!"

Outside the great windows, night had fallen.

Stars hung in the dark tropical sky, brilliant in their light. The *Aurora*, sound and whole, frisked in the evening breeze as if she were a living creature, and glad to be alive.

Captain Hunter put his hand on my uncle's forearm and gave it a friendly shake. "Come on, Patch," he said with a grin. "We broke up Steele's armada, and now Barrel will give a good report of us to his master. Take my word for it, the plan is unfolding well. We'll live yet to see Jack Steele go down to Davy Jones's locker."

"I hope so," my uncle said. He glanced my way and softly repeated, "I hope so."

And knowing I was the one for whom he wished all the good fortune in the world, I looked down at my plate and did not speak.

Sometimes I think I am the biggest fool alive.

Pirate Hunter 2:
The Guns of Tortuga

Much of this book is based on truth. The golden age of piracy in the Caribbean began in the 1600s. Spain claimed all of the West Indies, Central America, and most of South America. In the opinion of the king of Spain, no other nations had any right to send ships to these areas.

But the Spanish settlers in the colonies did not want to pay the high prices that Spain charged for goods and supplies. The colonists eagerly traded with Portuguese, French, Dutch, and English ships. To the authorities in Spain, these were pirate vessels. The traders, though, thought they were performing a service for the colonies and making a living for themselves.

On the island of Tortuga, north of what is today Haiti, a group of tough cattle drovers sprang up in the early 1600s. These men hunted wild cattle or raised and slaughtered domesticated cattle to provide meat for the Spanish and other sailors. Because they smoked the meat on frames called boucans, these men, mostly French, became known as boucaniers. The English called them buccaneers. When English leaders like Sir Henry Morgan set out to make war against the Spanish, they recruited these rough buccaneers as soldiers. Morgan was a privateer himself. He had a commission from the governor of Jamaica that allowed him to fight the enemies of the king of England, including the Spanish.

But the Spanish considered Morgan and his buccaneers pirates, of course. By the time of our story, 1687, Spain had signed treaties with the French, Dutch, and English. As part of the treaty agreements, the governments were supposed to disband the buccaneer groups. Many of these men had grown accustomed to their plundering way of life, and they had no intention of changing. The difference was that, without their governments' permission to attack Spanish ships and colonies, now the buccaneers were outlaws. These were the true pirates. Even Sir Henry Morgan, an old buccaneer himself, worked to hunt down these pirates and to bring peace to the West Indes.

It took many years. The high point of piracy in American waters was between the late 1680s and about 1740. The names of the pirates of that time are still well known: Calico Jack Rackham, Anne Bonney and Mary Reade (two women pirates!), Major Stede Bonnet, Captain William Kidd, and of course Edward Teach—Blackbeard. Our Jack Steele is a little like them. He is different, too, because most American pirates sailed small vessels, sloops or brigs, and were loners. Jack Steele, a natural leader, sails a mighty warship and is seeking to become the Pirate King of the New World.

So although our tale is fiction, it has roots in the truth. Piracy was not a fun occupation. It was dangerous, cruel, and dirty, and most pirates had short careers and short lives. Still, they were men who liked freedom and who hated the life of ordinary sailors. A Royal

Navy sailor could expect bad food, hard work, and whippings for every mistake or every minor violation of a rule. Their pay was often months or even years late in coming. And merchant sailors had it even worse! At least a Royal Navy captain usually gave no more than one or two dozen lashes as punishment. A private captain could order any number. Some of them forced sick men to climb the rigging and work the sails, even though the effort sometimes killed the suffering sailors. When we read about such true stories and thought about the pirates of the West Indies, it seemed to us that the strange thing was not that honest sailors sometimes turned pirate. Odder still was that most of them did not!

Welcome to the world of pirates and pirate hunting. It is a rugged world, and it does not have much glamour in it. But it offers excitement and adventure, and even humor of a kind. We hope you enjoy the voyage!

—Brad Strickland and Thomas E. Fuller
FEBRUARY 2002

BRAD STRICKLAND has written or cowritten nearly fifty novels. He and Thomas E. Fuller have worked together on many books about Wishbone, TV's literature-loving dog, and Brad and his wife Barbara have also written books featuring Sabrina, the Teenage Witch, the mystery-solving Shelby Woo, and characters from *Star Trek*. On his own, Brad has written mysteries, science fiction, and fantasy novels. When he is not writing, Brad is a professor of English at Gainesville College in Oakwood, Georgia. He and Barbara have a daughter, Amy, a son, Jonathan, and a daughter-in-law, Rebecca. They also have a house full of pets, including two dogs, three cats, a ferret, a gerbil, and two goldfish, one named George W. Bush and one named Fluffy.

THOMAS E. FULLER has been coauthoring young-adult novels with Brad Strickland for the last five years. They are best known for their work on the Wishbone mysteries as well as a number of radio dramas and published short stories. Otherwise, Thomas is best known as the head writer of the Atlanta Radio Theatre Company. He has won awards for his adaptation of H. G. Wells's *The Island of Dr. Moreau*, his original drama "The Brides of Dracula," and the occult western "All Hallow's Moon." Thomas lives in Duluth, Georgia, in a slightly shabby blue house full of books, manuscripts, audio tapes, and too many children including his sons Edward, Anthony, and John and occasionally his daughter, Christina.

READ ON FOR A PREVIEW OF THE NEXT
ADVENTURES OF CAPTAIN HUNTER AND
THE CREW OF THE *AURORA* IN

Heart of Steele

"A SHIP!"

The cry came drifting down from the maintop, almost like a leaf falling from a canvas tree. I lifted my head from the coil of rope where I lay dozing. The air felt hot and heavy, as it had been for more than a week. What breeze there was barely served to move the frigate *Aurora* forward. It was the summer of 1688 and the Caribbees simmered like a buccaneer's barbeque.

"On deck, there! A ship!"

The cry came again and I squinted up the tall stepped lines of the mainmast to where wiry old Abel Tate stood watch in the crow's nest. Around me I could hear other members of the *Aurora*'s crew bestirring themselves, struggling up from where they had lain languid in the heat. It was all I could do to haul myself to my feet, but the idea of anything that might offer escape from the usual dreaded doldrums finally got me out of my comfortable coil. I staggered over to where my friend Mr. Jeffers, the gunner, stood, shading his single good eye from the sun with one callused hand.

"Devil can I see a thing," he muttered. "It could be whale, rock, or ship for I might swear!" Even with the sweat pouring into my own eyes, I had to smile. If he were aiming his beloved cannons, Mr. Jeffers had the eyes of a sea eagle. Otherwise he was a blind as a bat in a well.

I heard the stamp of boots on the quarterdeck above us and two voices—one light and laughing, the other rumbling and complaining. The laughing voice belonged to our captain, Mad William Hunter, the noted pirate hunter. The grumbling one was that of my uncle, Patrick Shea, the noted surgeon and pessimist. Once they clapped eyes on me, the two would think of one thousand and one errands and chores to keep me from anything dangerous—or interesting. I grasped an idea and felt energy start to flow back into my sweat-drenched body. Uncle Patch says idle hands are the devil's workshop. That may be, but it takes a bit of inspiration to actually use the tools.

"Perhaps it just takes a younger eye, Mr. Jeffers," I said in my most innocent voice—which never seemed to fool anyone for some reason. Mr. Jeffers turned and raised one ragged eyebrow in my direction. "And, of course, a bit of height." I let my own eyes drift upward. Mr. Jeffers's gaze followed my gaze, and a broad grin spread across his scarred face.

"Aye, Davy, lad! Up ye go and send us back true word! That fool Tate would be sighting London Bridge if he thought he could!"

Quick as thought, I was out of my shoes and scurrying up the mainmast shrouds, my toes clutching the ratlines as I climbed. I heard a distant bellow that could have been Uncle Patch—or a bear amazed to find itself at sea. As long as I didn't look down, I could honestly say I couldn't tell which. So I climbed on and the gun deck of the *Aurora* fell away beneath me.

The higher I rose, the stronger the breezes driving our ship forward became. After the humid listlessness of the past weeks, it felt like a swim in a cold river. I found myself climbing faster and faster until at least I reached Abel Tate in his lofty perch atop the great central mainmast.

"What's the news, Mr. Tate?" I gasped out, drawing the cool air into my laboring lungs. "Mr. Jeffers has sent me up to find out what's what."

"Figured it wasn't the cap'n," he grumbled back. "Cap'n Hunter's got two good eyes in his head. Bartholomew Jeffers couldn't see the end of his own nose with a spyglass!" He turned and grinned at me. "Course, a good glass might help someone else to use the good sight God gave them."

With that, he slapped his own glass into my hands and pointed carefully off to starboard. "There lies a bark, Davy, where the sea meets sky, or I'm a Barbary ape, I am!"

Quickly I extended the glass and scanned the horizon where his finger pointed, straight off the starboard bow. It took a second or two for my eye to adjust and a few after that to find her, but there she was, on the far horizon and low in the water. Too low.

"No wonder Mr. Jeffers couldn't see her," I cried. "All her masts are down!"

"Aye, 'twas only pure luck that I spied her in the first place! Not a stump above her railings. Could have been a reef for all she showed!"

"Could she have wrecked in a storm, Mr. Tate?"

"If storm it was, she had it all to herself, she did! Not a hint of wind did we have until this morning! You tell the cap'n it weren't no storm that stripped her. He has the word of Abel Tate on that!"

I started to fly back down the lines, as fast as I could move hands and feet. If no storm had dismasted that lonely hulk on the horizon than only one other thing could have:

Pirates.

Test your detective skills with these spine-tingling Aladdin Mysteries!

The Star-Spangled Secret
By K. M. Kimball

Mystery at Kittiwake Bay
By Joyce Stengel

Scared Stiff
By Willo Davis Roberts

O'Dwyer & Grady
Starring in Acting Innocent
By Eileen Heyes

Ghosts in the Gallery
By Barbara Brooks Wallace

The York Trilogy By Phyllis Reynolds Naylor

Shadows on the Wall

Faces in the Water

Footprints at the Window